BEAU RIVAGE

Books by Margaret MacWilliams

BEAU RIVAGE
MISTRAL

BEAU RIVAGE

MARGARET MACWILLIAMS

DOUBLEDAY & COMPANY, INC.

GARDEN CITY, NEW YORK

1983

All of the characters in this book
are fictitious, and any resemblance
to actual persons, living or dead,
is purely coincidental.

Library of Congress Cataloging in Publication Data

MacWilliams, Margaret.
Beau Rivage.
I. Title.
PS3563.A3384B4   1983   8136.54
ISBN: 0-385-19066-2

First Edition

Library of Congress Catalog Card Number

Dedicated to my granddaughter Zoë

BEAU RIVAGE

CHAPTER 1

Carol Spencer leaned against the low stone balustrade which bordered the terrace of Beau Rivage. Two hundred feet beneath her the Caribbean stretched westward, its surf washing rhythmically against the black volcanic sand of the beach—a beach created untold centuries ago, carved out of the jagged promontories of the coast of Martinique by the relentless, ceaseless pounding of the sea.

The village of Belle Fontaine, nestled far below, was so meticulously assembled that from a distance it resembled a toy settlement instead of the dwelling place of hardworking fishermen. Its red tile roofs were a startling contrast to the brilliant blue waters beyond and the backdrop of lush tropical foliage.

Entranced by the scene, she could readily understand why this island in the windward group of the Antilles had been christened "L'Île des Revenants"—"The Isle Where People Come Back," and why some years ago her father had selected it, content to spend his productive years there, writing novels that had given him worldwide renown.

"It must be difficult to be the daughter of Carl Spencer!" This was a comment which had been made all too frequently by well-meaning friends and acquaintances, and unwilling to reply frankly, she had developed a stock innocuous answer, not revealing that she had never considered him her father.

He had been married four times, deserting his first wife, her mother, soon after she was born, and the wound had cut far too deeply to be discussed with even her most intimate companions.

Now Carl Spencer had died and to her astonishment had left her this legacy—Beau Rivage. It remained a mystery why he had done so, for his attorney in New York had remained vague and laconic regarding her father's motives, summoning her to his office to state that as Beau Rivage belonged to her, it might be prudent to travel to Martinique to view her inheritance.

Completely dazed by his startling revelation, she had listened numbly, barely absorbing his words while he explained that as the executor of the estate he had been instructed to pay all future taxes on the property as well as the salaries of a Creole couple who had taken care of Beau Rivage from the time Carl Spencer had purchased it.

"I visited Beau Rivage once," he told her, "shortly before your father's death. I went to revise his will, as a matter of fact. You see, you weren't included in the original. It's quite a distance from Fort-de-France, and as the villa has been temporarily put in mothballs, you'd be wise to stay in the city for a day or two. I'll write to the Larousses, the couple who worked for him, to inform them that you'll be arriving soon. Fort-de-France has plenty of first-rate hotels, but as it's Carnival time, I suggest you make reservations at once through your travel agent—that is if you follow my advice and decide to look over the property."

That had been the conclusion of her meeting with her father's attorney. To her it seemed incredible that it had taken place less than a week ago. Still slightly disoriented by the long flight from Kennedy and the hazardous taxi ride along the coastal road from Fort-de-France, with a shake of her head to dislodge the persistent dreamlike quality which surrounded her, she turned from her contemplation of Belle Fontaine and the sea to investigate her property.

The terrace of faded rose bricks was shaded by giant mango trees. At the far end she saw an oval pool fed with water from a mountain stream which plunged over the steep cliff to the beach below—the rushing water made the only sound to break the stillness of a late afternoon in February.

The house of ancient vintage was built of mahogany, weathered to a silvery gray by the trade winds from the Caribbean. Luxuriant bougainvillea, tinted from royal purple and red to delicate lavender, tumbled from the balcony on the second floor to the wide veranda below. The red tile roof was softened by a covering of moist green lichen.

Gingerly she entered the building, finding it was dark and cool inside, the jalousied windows shutting out the sunlight. The large living room was tastefully furnished with bamboo chairs and tables, its whitewashed walls massed with flamboyant paintings of tropical flowers.

She wandered from there to a smaller room which she realized must have been her father's study. A long, sturdily built table stood by the open windows, a covered typewriter resting on its highly polished surface. It was bereft of books and manuscripts, but a white envelope and a framed photograph were carefully placed in the center.

Overcome by curiosity she circled the table and to her surprise saw her own image staring back at her. Her hands trembled as she lifted the picture and moved to the window for a closer examination. It was the photograph she had selected for her college year book. There she was, leaning casually against a tree on the campus, wearing jeans and a white blouse, her long blond hair gently tousled by a breeze, her wide-set gray eyes, serious and unsmiling, looking straight into the camera.

"So he didn't forget me after all," she said softly, carefully placing the photograph back on the table as she realized that the envelope beside it was addressed to her in a bold, dashing scrawl. Settling herself in an easy chair by the window, she eagerly broke the seal. It was dated December 1980, shortly before his death.

"Carol," it began. "I do not have the brashness or insensitivity to address you as Dear Carol or Dear Daughter, for I am fully aware I long ago abrogated the right. Your short story which appeared recently in the *Atlantic Monthly* has been brought to my attention, and although you have a long way to go on the perilous road to becoming a writer—and I warn you that it is a lonely road replete with pitfalls and disappointments—I recognized an unusual talent. Lord knows the world today is in need of it. I have been told that I have not much longer to live. Therefore, passing the torch onto to you, I bequeath you Beau Rivage. Here, I trust, you will find tranquillity and solitude in pursuing the path you have chosen. Good luck and God bless." It was signed, Carl Spencer.

The letter fell to the floor. Her eyes clouded with sudden tears as for the first time in her twenty-three years, she felt close to her father, causing some of the resentment toward him to be dissipated. Of course, he had not been totally heartless. He had not left her mother completely adrift and poverty stricken. Through his attorney a generous monthly allowance had been sent, which had guaranteed a comfortable living, but this had failed to alleviate her mother's bitterness, which had been transmitted to her at an early age.

With a brief apology to her mother, who had died during her senior year at Smith, she felt a spark of love toward Carl Spencer, who in the last analysis, in his own unorthodox manner, had not only acknowledged her as his daughter but had given her the opportunity to continue her timorous attempts to write.

I won't go back to Boston, at least not for a while, she told herself with rising excitement, for if I'm careful I have enough money saved to eke out a living.

She heard the impatient blast of the horn from her waiting taxi and rising from the chair by the window, she called out, "I'm coming."

She had not turned on a light. It had become dusky in the small study. She stumbled against the desk and as a light flashed on she heard a deep masculine voice declare, "I'm curious to see if you resemble your father."

Cramming the letter into the pocket of her seersucker traveling suit, she stared wordlessly at the stranger standing in the doorway.

"Not a bit," he said, approaching her. He had the temerity to tilt her chin upward, examining her face more closely. "Which is probably a good thing," he continued, "for not even his most ardent admirers could have called him handsome. Incidentally, I like blond hair even when it is a trifle untidy. On second thought, however, your eyes do resemble his—gray, intelligent and more often than not alive with a zest for living. His most attractive feature."

She jerked away from him, repelled by his audacity, disconcerted by the overpowering aura of masculinity which crackled like lightning in the room. She had a jumbled impression of luminous dark eyes, a burnished complexion and a lissome body, momentarily quiescent but with latent qualities of virility and vigor.

"Who are you?" she demanded, furious to discover that her voice quavered.

He moved back a step, slipping his hands into the pockets of his white shorts. "Forgive me," he replied easily. "I'm forgetting my manners. I am Jules Saint Laurent, your father's neighbor. Although I must admit Carl Spencer never became overly friendly, we did spend some pleasant evenings together. He spoke of you now and then, but he failed to mention you were beautiful. Quite an oversight on his part, don't you think?"

Flushing she replied heatedly, "I never knew my father. Now if you will excuse me, Mr. Saint Laurent, it is late and my taxi is waiting." As she spoke a second impatient honk sounded outside.

With a curt shake of her head, she brushed past him, ignoring his proffered hand, irritated by his possessive manner. "I suspect," she said coldly, "that as a result of this first encounter, you will find me more aloof than my father, for I haven't the least desire to develop a neighborly relationship."

He laughed, his strong white teeth flashing as he opened the door to the veranda, waiting for her to precede him. "You misunderstand me," he said. "I too have no wish for a neighborly relationship, or any relationship at all, for that matter. I'm here purely on business. You see, I desire to purchase Beau Rivage."

"Beau Rivage is not for sale," she snapped back.

They faced each other on the veranda, resembling two warriors about to engage in mortal combat. She noticed that his hands were clenched, that he was no longer smiling, until without warning, like a chameleon, he became once more insouciant and relaxed.

"A pity," he replied lightly. "But perhaps when my attorney approaches you with a splendid offer, you'll change your mind."

He gave her no opportunity to reply as with a lithe movement he turned and strode purposefully across the brick terrace, disappearing among the thick foliage beyond the pool.

The taxi honked once more and with a determined thrust of her chin, she hurried across the terrace to the gravel driveway. "Sorry," she said apologetically, climbing into the rear seat and sinking against the worn-out upholstery with a sigh of relief.

"Where to, missy?" the Creole driver asked, turning on the motor, which coughed and sputtered in such a fashion that she doubted if they would successfully complete the return trip to Fort-de-France.

"L'Impératrice," she replied, closing her eyes as he barreled off at a frightening pace along the narrow, twisting road, apparently inured to the hazardous hairpin turns and the steep ridges that plunged downward precipitously to the rocky coast.

"Do you know of a Jules Saint Laurent?" she asked, her curiosity finally overcoming her fear that her last hour on earth was just around the next bend in the road.

He nodded his head vigorously, further alarming her by turning around to favor her with a broad grin. Neatly dressed in jeans and a dark blue shirt, he spoke in a steady stream of patois, which was completely foreign to her ears.

"S'il vous plaît," she interrupted him, struggling to recall her schoolgirl French. *"En anglais, si possible, monsieur."*

With a tremendous effort, he answered laboriously. "M. Saint Laurent is great man, much land at Belle Fontaine. Known in Fort-de-France, in Saint Pierre, everywhere."

"I see." Realizing he had exhausted his repertoire, Carol Spencer closed her eyes and offered a brief prayer to her Maker to spare her life from an untimely end, not stirring until the taxi driver delivered her unscathed at the welcoming entrance of the Hôtel l'Impératrice.

CHAPTER 2

The Hôtel l'Impératrice commanded a splendid view of the waterfront of Fort-de-France. They arrived at the fleeting moment before darkness descends when objects are depicted with sharp clarity, as though night is offering one final chance to view the world before she lowers her impenetrable curtain.

Despite her weariness, Carol paused on the threshold, bemused by what she saw as her luggage was unloaded and carried inside by an efficient bellhop.

In the harbor a large cruise ship lay at anchor. Another was tethered to the dock. Aglow from bow to stern, their lights shimmered on the darkening waters, while the massive stone bastions of Fort Saint Louis brooded above them, a stern reminder that once Martinique had witnessed violent clashes between France and her long-standing enemy, Great Britain.

The scene was alive with tourists, jostled good naturedly by Martiniquais, the passengers from the cruise ships either going or coming from the narrow side streets crammed with boutiques, offering Dior neckties, Hermès scarfs and Chanel perfume.

It had the flavor of Paris when she had visited there during her junior year at college, while the coastal road she had recently traversed recalled the glamorous Côte d'Azur,

with its breathtaking curves and brief, tantalizing glimpses
of the Mediterranean at the base of the craggy cliffs.

In the lobby she threaded her way to the reservation desk
and soon was guided to her room. With a view of the
waterfront, it was a large airy place with a huge four-poster
bed in the center. Mosquito netting was fastened to the
ceiling, festooning the bed like a circus tent. Before changing for dinner, she stepped outside onto the balcony, drink-
ing in the fast, exciting tempo of the city, still finding it
difficult to believe that she was the owner of a charming villa
in Martinique with the time to explore this enchanting
island from its southern to its northern tip.

I'll be able to write here, she thought with deep satisfaction. I'll give myself one year. Certainly with almost five
thousand dollars in the bank, I can make ends meet. Silently,
she thanked her father for arranging to pay the taxes and the
wages of two servants, who would not only free her from
household chores but introduce her to the customs and
mores of her new environment.

She bathed and dressed leisurely, slipping into a light blue
silk frock, and as she took one last look in the mirror, she
recalled that Jules Saint Laurent had pronounced her beautiful. She was forced to concede, although he was obviously
prone to exaggeration, that she was not ashamed of her
appearance. From her mother she had inherited a flawless,
creamy complexion and luxuriant, glistening blond hair,
while her wide-set gray eyes, so like her father's, were arresting, containing a hint of mystery, a need to conceal her
innermost thoughts.

She had always understood why Carl Spencer, a young
and struggling writer, had fallen in love with her mother.
She had been a soft-spoken Southern belle, vivacious and

flirtatious with a kaleidoscopic personality that had captured her father, only to soon disillusion him. Yet it was not entirely his fault, she thought, now reluctantly willing to acknowledge that her mother had been ill equipped to be tied to a temperamental, serious writer who admittedly could be irascible and more often than not difficult to handle.

Recalling his three other wives, whom she had never met but had read about extensively, she decided that Carl Spencer undoubtedly had one characteristic in common with Jules Saint Laurent in that he probably should never have married, and if Jules Saint Laurent had already acquired a wife, she was to be pitied.

Realizing that she was starved, Carol pulled a silk scarf from her suitcase, threw it over one arm and clutching her purse descended to the first floor in search of the dining room.

It was dimly lit and overflowing with tourists; she was fortunate to find a vacant table in a far corner of the room. Harsh American voices dominated the salon, almost extinguishing the muted patois of the natives, and as she studied the menu, she vowed not only to brush up on her French but to attempt to master the Creole language of the islanders, whose cadences, since the long-ago days of Louis XIII, had been softened and blurred by the steady influx of Africans.

"Good evening, Mlle. Spencer."

The voice was that of a Frenchman, fluent in English but with an unmistakable accent. Startled, Carol looked up and saw she was being addressed by a dapper gray-haired gentleman, meticulously turned out in a white suit, his most outstanding features a neat well-clipped moustache and dark eyes, keen and perceptive.

"How do you know my name?" she asked with a puzzled frown.

"Quite simple. The concierge at the desk informed me you were having dinner and described you as a young, attractive lady, so it was not difficult to single you out from the crowd." With a Gallic shrug of his shoulders, he flicked his eyes across the dining room jammed with middle-aged and elderly Americans.

"May I introduce myself?" he continued smoothly. "I am Jacques Despard, an attorney for Jules Saint Laurent. Very possibly his name is unfamiliar to you, but not for long. His property borders Beau Rivage and he is most interested in—"

"He is most interested in purchasing it," Carol Spencer broke in as he pulled out a chair across from her and without permission sat down.

"Oh, you have already met him—when?"

"This afternoon. I couldn't wait to see Beau Rivage. My father's lawyer in New York had given me a set of keys. I went directly there from the airport."

"Ah—a beautiful place, in addition to being a valuable piece of property."

"Which I do not intend to sell," she replied succinctly, tossing him a challenging glance.

"Later, perhaps, you will allow me to discuss the matter further, but not before you have dinner." He spoke mildly with a wry twist to his lips. "You will discover that food in Martinique is superb, to be enjoyed in a leisurely fashion. Am I wrong in my assumption that my friend Jules approached you this afternoon in his usual forthright manner, upsetting you to some degree? He lacks tact, that young man, but what he lacks in one area, he makes up with his charm. Don't you agree?"

"I failed to find him charming," Carol replied caustically.

"A pity! Most women do." He turned to the waiter who was hovering near them, addressing him rapidly in patois. As the waiter scurried off he said, "I have taken the liberty to order the island's favorite punch—smooth white rum laced with sugar syrup with the juice of limes. Guaranteed to calm the nerves as well as ruffled tempers. Will you join me?"

Carol, amused by the droll expression on his face, found herself agreeing that not only would she sample the punch but he would be in sole charge of ordering her first dinner in Martinique.

The punch more than lived up to his promise, lessening her irritation over this apparently concerted effort to pressure her to sell her property. The meal was equally delectable as turtle soup was served, garnished with a floating turtle egg, followed by lobster, creamed chicken and rice accompanied by tiny loaves of French bread, a green salad, assorted cheeses and finally French pastries as light as a feather.

They shared a bottle of wine and by the time the café noir was presented in silver cups, Carol had momentarily forgotten her confrontation with Jules Saint Laurent, which had struck an unpleasant note in an otherwise perfect day.

As she sipped the strong coffee, her eyes traveled around the room. She was amused to see that many of the American women must have spent the afternoon shopping, for they were wearing madras headdresses, colorful turbans in brilliant colors with one end sticking up like a plume.

M. Despard, observing her interest, launched into an explanation of an old native custom, his eyes filled with mirth. "Little do they know," he remarked, "what a madras turban with one point indicates."

"What does it indicate?" Carol asked, her curiosity aroused.

"It means, I am free and available."

Carol chuckled. "Are these ladies unaware of that?"

"Probably, but it is merely a harmless joke, played upon them by some shopkeeper. Now two points mean, I am promised so don't waste your time. Three points proclaim, I am a happily married woman, stay away from me."

"And four points?" Carol asked.

"I'm not free, yet I'm interested."

"Well," Carol remarked, "If I meet Jules Saint Laurent again, I'll be certain not to wear a turban with one point. However, none of the others seem to fit my category."

"Free but not available?" he ventured.

"Exactly."

"Then we must introduce a new headdress with five points for you," he replied.

With an equable expression he sipped his café noir and asked for permission to light a cigar. "Speaking of Jules Saint Laurent," he said, "will you allow me to at least mention the offer he intends to make? You see, I promised him I would follow through. It would be most embarrassing if I failed to honor my commitment."

"Of course, although my answer will still be no. Tell me, why is he anxious to own Beau Rivage?"

"It's rather a lengthy tale." M. Despard relaxed comfortably in his chair, obviously enjoying his cigar and the after-dinner liqueur he had ordered. "I'll make it as brief as possible. For many years Beau Rivage belonged to the Saint Laurent family. It was their ancestral home, a part of the sugar plantation, which Jules owns and operates. Today he is a wealthy man, but for his family that has not always been the case. There was a period when crops were extremely poor, and his father to prevent bankruptcy was forced to sell Beau Rivage to your father. When times improved, they built a large home on the plantation where Jules lives. But he has never become reconciled to losing Beau Rivage. He wants it back. Surprisingly, despite the fact that he is an astute businessman, he possesses a sentimental streak."

"Strange—this afternoon M. Saint Laurent did not strike me as a sentimentalist."

"Oh, but he is, at least as far as Beau Rivage is concerned. He is also thoroughly convinced that eventually he will attain his goal."

"Beau Rivage is one goal he will not attain," Carol said firmly, thinking at the same time that if she proved to be a failure in the field of writing, which could very conceivably occur, Beau Rivage might appear on the market, forcing her to eat humble pie.

"What is he prepared to pay?" she finally asked, anxious to be courteous to M. Despard and allow him to make good his promise to his client. "I'm interested to learn how far this sentimentality goes."

"Very far indeed." Monsieur spoke dryly. "One million five hundred francs to be precise, which translated into American money means roughly three hundred thousand dollars."

"That much!" Carol gasped.

"You are impressed?" There was a gleam of hope in Monsieur's intelligent dark eyes, which was immediately doused when Carol shook her head replying.

"I'm impressed, yes, but the answer still remains no. You

see, M. Despard, I've fallen in love with Beau Rivage. I too am sentimental. It was where my father wrote his novels that brought him fame. I hope to follow in his footsteps and be a successful writer too. In his last letter, my father wished me well, asking me to carry on the torch for him, so you can understand that in a way I am committed. I have no desire to let him down. Besides, even if I were anxious to sell, M. Saint Laurent's attitude this afternoon would have spurred me on to defy him. I dislike being pushed around."

"Ah, me," Monsieur sighed. "You are as stubborn as he. But let me warn you, Jules will not give up easily. He will persist."

"Then please tell him for me that the more he persists, the more I will continue to resist!" Carol's gray eyes flashed with anger.

The dining room was slowly emptying. Their waiter stood nearby failing to conceal his impatience for their departure.

"We seem to have reached an impasse," Jacques Despard said soberly.

Carol nodded. "Yes, I agree." Unable to stifle a yawn, she gathered up her scarf and purse. "It's been a long, tiring day, but a wonderful one. Thank you so much for the excellent dinner, M. Despard. It was a marvelous introduction to Martinique."

He escorted her to the elevator, giving her a courtly bow before departing. As she watched him cross the lobby of l'Impératrice, stepping out into the still teeming sidewalks of Fort-de-France, she wondered when he would inform Jules Saint Laurent of her refusal, of her determination that Beau Rivage was not for sale.

In her dimly lit room, the wide four-poster bed was most inviting. Nothing, she knew, could prevent her from a long trouble-free sleep. As she undressed, she speculated as to how Jules Saint Laurent would receive her message. She imagined he possessed a fiery temper when aroused. She hoped that at this very moment he was pacing around his plantation house thoroughly out of sorts and frustrated.

Fastening a white silk robe around her slim waist, she was drawn to the balcony by the sounds of Carnival, which all during dinner had been a backdrop to her conversation with M. Despard and now were reaching a crescendo.

The street was jammed with Martiniquais, the women flamboyant in their native costumes. A float festooned with tropical flowers had paused beneath her window, and on its tiny platform a young couple moved with grace to the beat of a calypso band.

The crowd, caught up in the persuasive rhythm, began to clap their hands while the tempo of the steel drums increased in speed and intensity until finally the dancers, breathless and laughing, collapsed into each other's arms, to be carried off and replaced by another couple, who circled the float this time with slow sensuous movements, by their gestures wordlessly, delicately wooing each other.

She stood there on the balcony for some time, entranced by the pageantry, by the lively childlike mood of the crowd, unable despite her weariness to think of sleep.

Later when the float moved on and people began to disperse, the music becoming soft and muted, she stretched out between the cool sheets of her four-poster bed, puzzling over M. Despard's remark that his client would persist until he attained his objective. Was it a carefully veiled warning of future confrontations? she wondered.

Yawning as she plumped up her pillows, she decided that she would not allow herself to be disturbed by any challenge,

CHAPTER 3

Carol Spencer swam back and forth with an easy rhythmical stroke across the pool on the terrace of Beau Rivage. The intense tropical sun turned the water into an iridescent mirror, while the sound of the mountain stream which tumbled over the cliff to the beach below mingled with the clamorous chant of the birds in the treetops.

Pulling herself out of the pool, she rested on the edge for some time until fearful of becoming burned, she stretched out on a deck chair under the protective shade of a mango tree. It was midafternoon and as she closed her eyes drifting into a delightful half sleep, she relived the events of what had developed into a momentous day.

After a continental breakfast, she had checked out of the Hôtel l'Impératrice risking another hazardous taxi ride along the coastal road toward Belle Fontaine. This time she arrived at Beau Rivage to the hum of a vacuum cleaner accompanied by warm greetings from M. and Mme. Larousse, who apologized profusely for not having learned of her arrival until that morning.

The Larousses were a middle-aged couple, dark skinned, with the melting chocolate-brown eyes characteristic of their race, and empathy was immediately established between them and Carol. Annette Larousse, a plump energetic matron attired in a bright yellow dress, escorted her with great ceremony through the house, first to the spotless kitchen replete with glistening copper pots and pans and the latest culinary equipment.

"M. Spencer enjoyed good cooking," she explained, and there was no question in Carol's mind but that Annette Larousse was eminently qualified to provide it.

She was relieved to discover that the Larousses, under the tutelage of her father, had mastered English remarkably well and there would be no difficulty in communicating.

The dining room in the rear of the building opened onto a wide veranda, providing a view of the garden, its rich soil teeming with delicate orchids, flaming anthuriums and the ostentatious blossoms of birds-of-paradise. Beyond, Annette pointed with pride to a neat white cottage partially concealed by bougainvillea. "M. Spencer built it for us," she explained. "He was a kind, considerate gentleman."

There were four spacious bedrooms on the second floor with high, beamed ceilings and mosaic tile floors intricately designed in blue and gold patterns. The master bedroom, the most pretentious, opened onto a balcony overlooking the terrace, its lacy wrought-iron railing reminiscent of the Vieux Carré in New Orleans. It offered a splendid view of the sea, which on this matchless morning lay motionless, so intense in coloration that it resembled a painting by Gauguin.

The huge four-poster bed, covered with the inevitable netting, took up a large part of the room, while the modern bathroom adjoining it made it clear that Carl Spencer had spared no expense to provide his establishment with the latest conveniences, at the same time carefully retaining its unique Caribbean flavor.

"You like?" Annette Larousse had inquired anxiously.

"Oh, yes. It's perfect," Carol had exclaimed.

Étienne Larousse, his face deeply wrinkled from years spent under the torrid sun, was in charge of handling the outside tasks. He guided her through the lush garden to the garage, where her father's Renault was lodged.

"No more taxis," she said with a laugh of relief as she inspected the venerable vehicle, its chrome polished until it glowed, obviously Étienne's most prized possession. He proudly assured her that despite its age, it purred like a contented kitten on the highway.

Protesting that she was being thoroughly spoiled, she had lunched on the terrace enjoying "calalu," a thick soup flavored with dark green leaves, accompanied by red wine and slices of fresh pineapple.

She was drifting into a delicious slumber when she was rudely awakened by a voice that had since yesterday become all too familiar, instantly destroying the serenity of her lazy afternoon siesta.

"Jacques Despard tells me your answer is no," he said without preamble, remarkably unconcerned that he was not only trespassing but interrupting her pleasant dreams.

"He warned me that you would be persistent." Reluctantly she forced open her drowsy eyelids, staring at him with dislike. "Why don't you go away!" she declared in a disgruntled voice.

Unperturbed by her rebuff, he pulled a deck chair close to hers, stretched out on it slowly and deliberately, challenging her with an impish grin to ignore him. "We are neighbors, you know," he said with a disarming glance, "and neighbors should make an effort to get along. It can become very lonely in the country, Mlle. Spencer. It is, therefore, wise to cultivate those around you."

"I did not come here for that reason, M. Saint Laurent," she replied with asperity. "I came to be alone, to work without interruption."

"You didn't appear to be working very hard when I arrived." His dark eyes were carefully scrutinizing her body in her brief bikini. She blushed, wishing she had had the foresight to put on her beach robe, which she had left beside the pool.

"M. Saint Laurent," she said, enunciating each word slowly and distinctly so that he would not miss the portent of her caustic speech, "somehow I have gathered the impression that you consider every woman who happens to cross your path a willing victim to your charms."

"Ah, we are making progress. You admit I have charm."

"No such thing," she retorted angrily. Swinging her feet onto the warm bricks of the terrace, she tossed him a scornful glance as she strode away and picking up her beach robe gathered it around her. "You either misinterpret my words or pretend to misinterpret them. Last night I told your attorney that Beau Rivage was not for sale. He has obviously passed the information on to you. Therefore, why do you continue haunting me? Can't you see I find your company irritating? Can't you understand that I have no more interest in you than I have in—" She searched wildly for the proper conclusion, annoyed to discover that the hint of amusement in his dark eyes disconcerted and at the same time intrigued her. "I have no more interest in you than that frog over there who is about to jump into the pool," she finished lamely.

He was grinning again, a self-satisfied grin. She struggled against the temptation to stamp her foot in a thoroughly childish manner, which she well knew would serve to give him the upper hand in their ongoing contretemps.

"I find the word 'irritating' most encouraging," he said with maddening complacency. "Now I am certain that frog does not irritate you. He is merely something to engage your attention, to observe his antics and then forget him. If I irritate you, Mlle. Spencer, it means you are aware of me. An excellent start towards a closer relationship, don't you agree?"

"Closer relationship," Carol repeated icily. "You made it quite clear yesterday, M. Saint Laurent, that it was Beau Rivage you desire, not me. Why cloud the issue?"

"Because I've changed my mind." He was smiling broadly now, a smile that despite her determination to have nothing more to do with him aroused unsettling sensations deep within her.

"Yesterday after leaving you, I decided you were almost, not quite, but almost as desirable as your property." He moved across the terrace, touching her shoulder lightly and also her long blond hair, still wet and tangled from her recent swim. "Do you have any idea how scintillating you are when you're angry? Tell me, Carol. It must be Carol, for Mlle. Spencer is a far too formal address. Tell me, have you ever been in love?"

She wrenched away from him, dismayed that despite her valiant effort to maintain an impersonal approach, somehow he had succeeded in invading her privacy, exposing her as an amateur pitted against a professional.

As a result she revealed too much. "No, and I doubt if I ever will be. You must know enough about my father to guess that long ago he gave me a picture of marriage which has made the mere thought of it distasteful. I avoid the prospect of a permanent relationship with any man like the plague, whether he is an overbearing plantation owner in Martinique or an eligible bachelor in Boston."

He was laughing as he replied. "I am overcome by your naïveté. Who has spoken of a permanent relationship? Who has mentioned marriage? It was you, not I, for I am a loner too. Although I might some day ask you to become my mistress, I will never ask you to become my wife."

"Let me assure you, M. Saint Laurent, your mistress I will never be."

He shrugged his shoulders saying dolefully, "What a stubborn girl you are, Carol Spencer. You won't sell Beau Rivage. You won't contemplate the possibility of a temporary alliance, which I predict would be a delectable experience for both of us. In addition you have treated me in a most disparaging fashion, which intrigues rather than repels me. I'm always drawn towards what appears unattainable, and invariably discover that what I desire is attainable after all. Think about that for the rest of the day."

She watched him stride off as he had the afternoon before, without a backward glance.

"I trust this is good-bye, M. Saint Laurent," she called out as he disappeared into the thick shrubbery. If he had heard her final words, he vouchsafed no reply.

She was contemplating a plunge into the pool to wash away the lingering presence of Jules Saint Laurent when she saw a battered jeep plowing its way up the driveway, stopping at the edge of the terrace with a jerk and a protesting sputter.

"Hello!" A young woman at the wheel wigwagged to her as two children, a boy and a girl dressed in bathing togs, spilled onto the driveway, rambunctious and lively as puppies.

"Ann, Jeremy, calm down." She addressed them in a tone that implied her rebuke would not deter their antics. "I'm Betsy Johnson. These are my two wild Indians. I hope our visit isn't inconveniencing you."

Obviously in an advanced stage of pregnancy, which a voluminous jumper failed to conceal, she stretched out her hand in a friendly gesture of greeting. "Welcome to Beau Rivage. It's good to have a neighbor once more. We've missed Mr. Spencer dreadfully, especially the children, although I'll never know why he took a liking to them."

She had a broad face, liberally sprinkled with freckles. Her red hair, pulled back severely, was plaited into a thick braid down her back. At first Carol categorized her as extremely plain until she smiled and she sensed that here was a woman who could always be depended upon and once your friend would remain so for a lifetime.

"On the contrary, I'm glad you came. Do you live near here?" Carol beckoned to Betsy Johnson to join her on the terrace, wondering as she did why her father, who had never shown the slightest inclination to make her acquaintance, had apparently welcomed these two lively youngsters to Beau Rivage.

"We live a few miles north. No ocean view unfortunately, but we have a sweet place. My husband, David, works for a public relations firm in Fort-de-France. We've been here for three years and though I miss the States, on the whole I'm content. There's something about Martinique that gets in your blood. Have you felt the magic yet?"

"Yes, from the first moment I arrived."

Strolling together across the terrace, Carol smiled as she

watched the two children testing the water with their toes, challenging each other as to who should be the first to dive in. "They are good swimmers?" she asked anxiously.

"They swim like water babies." Betsy Johnson settled down heavily in a deck chair. "Actually, I've come to issue an invitation for tomorrow night for supper, strictly informal. Jules Saint Laurent and his latest flame will be there—by the way, his plantation adjoins your property—and I've asked Chad Anderson. He's a new arrival in Martinique and a little lonely. You'll like him, I think, and I know he'll like you." With frank admiration she was studying Carol's slender figure.

Carol frowned. "It sounds like fun," she said hesitantly. "Except for the presence of Jules Saint Laurent."

"You've met him already?" Betsy Johnson raised her eyebrows in surprise.

"Twice, unfortunately. As a matter of fact he left here seconds before your arrival. Both meetings have been, well, stormy. He wants to buy Beau Rivage and I have no intention of selling."

"I should think not!" Betsy exclaimed. "It's like Jules to attempt to snow you under with his demands. It's no secret, of course, that he considers Beau Rivage rightfully his. Ridiculous under the circumstances but there it is. Knowing Jules he won't give up easily. But don't be concerned about tomorrow. He's far too polite to be a controversial guest. Besides he'll be concentrating on Michelle La Roche, his latest conquest. She's the French prefect's daughter and a raging beauty."

"He's not married then?"

"Jules Saint Laurent married! Not a chance. He's too wedded to his sugar plantation to take a wife. Besides, he enjoys playing the part of Martinique's most eligible and elusive bachelor and hasn't the slightest inclination to change his status. Many have tried and failed in the past to marry him. I predict even the lovely Michelle with her smart Parisian clothes and old world charm will soon join the ranks of the vanquished."

"You've described him to perfection." Carol laughed, discovering to her relief that Betsy's candid, unflattering sketch of Jules Saint Laurent had served to place him in a proper perspective. No longer did he strike her as a threatening force, capable of destroying the tranquillity for which she was so ardently searching. Instead he had become slightly tiresome and ridiculous in his attempt to impress upon her that he was the conquering male, all powerful and irresistible. "I'll be happy to come to your party," she said enthusiastically. "Particularly if this Chad Anderson is a sane and sensible man who does not give the impression that he is planning and fully intends to seduce you."

"He's the opposite of Jules, if that's what you mean," Betsy said, causing Carol to shiver involuntarily at the memory of Jules' dark eyes boldly studying every contour of her well-assembled body while he touched her shoulder and her wet tangled hair as he had a short while ago, carelessly but with a disturbing intimacy.

When Annette Larousse appeared on the terrace with a tray of cool drinks, Betsy called out cheerily, "Annette, I've missed you. I trust Miss Spencer has discovered what a jewel she has acquired."

"I have," Carol agreed. "If lunch was a sample of her cooking, I'm in for a veritable windfall of gastronomic delights."

The children came out of the pool, racing across the

terrace to sample the drinks and gorge upon the French pastries that Annette had provided.

"What did you do before you came here?" Betsy asked after warning the children that two pastries apiece was the limit.

"I worked for a publishing house in Boston, sort of a gofer, the lowliest employee in the pecking order."

"You intend to return there?"

"I think not, for with probably more foolhardiness than discretion, I gave notice as soon as I learned my father had left me Beau Rivage. I plan to stay, to write, although to tell the truth, I feel I'm an interloper in this house, embarrassed to admit that I have the nerve to contemplate following in my father's footsteps."

"I don't see why not. He told me you had talent." Betsy shook her head, refusing the delectable array of pastries on the silver tray. "Weight problem," she said sorrowfully.

"My father spoke of me to you?" Carol asked eagerly.

"Yes, he did. Once. We were right here on this terrace watching the children swim. He confessed that for various reasons which he did not mention he had missed the chance to see his only child grow up. It was obvious he deeply regretted it. He spoke too of a story you had recently published, saying someday he believed your name would be as well known as his."

Carol's eyes filled with tears. "It's good to hear that," she murmured.

Betsy Johnson struggled out of her deck chair. "I'm awfully glad you're here," she said warmly. "It can be very lonely in Martinique, for after all, we are expatriates. I hope we will become good friends."

"I'm sure we will."

En rapport they strolled toward the jeep, the children lagging far behind them. "Come any day to swim," Carol offered. "If you hear my typewriter and I fail to appear, don't feel you're not welcome. Also I'm looking forward to tomorrow night."

"Around six o'clock." Betsy tossed her a bright smile, turning on the ignition. "Étienne knows the way. He'll drive you there and Chad can bring you home."

After they had left, Carol wandered into her father's study. Haltingly she removed the cover from his typewriter, surprised to see that it was a venerable Underwood. As she touched the keys tentatively, some of them stuck.

Opening the table drawer, she found it was filled with pens and paper. Remembering a biography of her father which had been a best seller, she recalled he had said that he was an old-fashioned writer who wrote his manuscript laboriously by hand, revising it many times before he finally resorted to his typewriter. She thought it strange that she had independently developed the same method.

A yellow tablet lay on top of the others, and in his now familiar handwriting he had scrawled on the first page, "Carol, don't be fearful of sitting at my desk."

Touched by his perceptiveness, feeling his presence in the room, she knew it was a friendly, encouraging presence, and with her anxiety, her nervousness allayed, she settled herself in his comfortable armchair and wrote the opening paragraph of her first novel.

CHAPTER 4

Working in her father's study, Carol completely forgot the passage of time until Annette brought dinner to her on a tray. "You are like your father," Annette remarked with a smile. "Often he stayed up until dawn."

In her anxiety not to stop the remarkable easy flow of words, she hardly let herself notice what she was eating. She was already familiar with the high peaks of accomplishment that come to a writer, all too frequently followed by dry, desultory periods when the proper phrases and sentences refuse to formulate, remaining in the background tantalizingly out of reach. It was close to sunrise when she showered and, slipping into a white silk negligee, stepped from her bedroom onto the balcony.

Since sundown she had heard the roar of the sea breaking on the rocks below accompanied by the steady patter of rain. Now she saw that the storm was over, the swollen gray clouds rolling away as if some celestial spirit had summoned them to disperse. She watched the sun, a huge red ball in the sky, calm the turbulent waters until the beat of the waves lessened.

The scene reminded her of Nag's Head on the Atlantic Coast where she and her mother had spent several summers, where her greatest thrill had been to challenge the towering waves as they crested and broke on the shore.

Descending to the terrace and leaning on the balustrade, she saw no one was about, the beach below deserted. Impulsively she picked her way down the steep stone steps, which had been carved out of the rocks, and when she reached the bottom, she wiggled her toes ecstatically in the wet, black sand. Glancing around to be certain she was alone, she tossed her robe onto a dry rock and plunged into the surf, diving cleanly through a breaker before it crested. Reaching calmer waters, she floated contentedly on her back.

"Are you mad?" a voice called out.

Treading water, she shaded her eyes to see who was addressing her in such a peremptory manner. Her predicament concerned her, for although her nakedness was protected by the waves, she was certainly in no position to swim ashore in the presence of a stranger.

Dismayed, she recognized Jules Saint Laurent standing in the shallow water, dressed in jeans rolled up to his knees, a fishing rod in his hand.

"I'm perfectly all right," she answered impatiently. "This is calm compared to the Atlantic."

"Nevertheless you'd better come in before you get a chill. Didn't you hear the storm last night? It's still too damn rough for a swim in the sea."

"I can't come in."

"Why on earth not?"

"I didn't bring along my bathing suit." She had drifted close enough to see the wicked grin on his face.

"How fortunate for me."

Surprised by a tremendous wave that buried her before tossing her a few feet from shore, she choked on a mouthful of seawater. "Please," she sputtered. "It is cold out here. Won't you turn your back or better yet go away?"

Unconcernedly he cast his line. "Why should I?" he asked. "I'm a busy man who arose early to engage in my favorite pastime. You swim while I fish."

As there was no doubt in her mind that the next breaker would dump her unceremoniously at his feet, she said, panic-stricken, "Please, do try to act like a gentleman."

"You gave me the impression yesterday that you didn't consider me a gentleman," he said, reeling in his line. "But I'll do what you ask on one condition."

"What is that?" Carol demanded, her voice revealing that she was about to experience a humiliating debacle to her morning escapade.

"That you'll invite me to breakfast on your terrace. The fish are ornery, refusing to bite, and I find I'm starved."

"All right," she agreed, relieved that his request was a mild one, for she had half-expected him to propose the sale of Beau Rivage as his price. "If you'll just turn around and face the cliffs, I'll be terribly obliged."

He turned his back as a wave toppled her on the wet sand. Gaining her footing, she raced to the rocks and flung her negligee around her, breathing heavily, her face flushed with embarrassment.

"Don't be alarmed," he said equably, "I've never ravished an unwilling female yet, although I must admit I'm tempted." His eyes raked her body from top to toe, and she was uncomfortably aware that her silk negligee clung to her wet skin in a most revealing manner.

"Thanks," she mumbled hurriedly, scrambling up the stone steps so swiftly that she stumbled and scraped her knee, infuriated to hear his laughter as she reached the safety of Beau Rivage.

She found Annette in the kitchen, startled by her bedraggled appearance. "I took a dip in the sea, Annette," she explained. "Unfortunately I ran into our neighbor, M. Saint Laurent. I promised him breakfast. Would you mind serving it to him on the terrace?" She yawned. "As for me, I plan to take a long sleep. I was up all night."

In the study, she tore off a sheet of paper from her notebook, wrote on it "Bon Appétit" and, handing it to Annette with a gleeful look, said, "Please see M. Saint Laurent finds this on his breakfast tray." She showered and, climbing into her comfortable four-poster bed, slept peacefully until late afternoon when it was time to dress for the Johnsons' supper party.

CHAPTER 5

Étienne drove Carol to the Johnsons' cottage, a modest dwelling, weathered like Beau Rivage to a silvery gray. Set on the edge of the rain forest, it blended into the landscape to such a degree that if one hadn't known it was there, it would have been easy to pass it by.

She was looking forward to the evening with mixed emotions, particularly since the early morning episode on the beach. It would be pleasant to see Betsy Johnson, to meet her husband and Chad Anderson, but the prospect of confronting Jules Saint Laurent disturbed her.

Three times they had met. Three times they had crossed swords, and she had reached the uncomfortable conclusion that so far he had emerged the winner. It was ridiculous, she thought, to be eager and at the same time reluctant to see him.

Annette, with a conspiratorial wink, had informed her that before he left Beau Rivage he had consumed a hearty breakfast, read her note without comment and had expressed the hope that Mlle. Spencer would suffer no ill effects from her early morning adventure.

Carol had interpreted this surprising equanimity as a peaceful interlude before the next storm, for his derisive laughter which had followed her as she ran helter-skelter up the stone steps to the terrace still echoed in her ears. Convinced that he well knew her feeble attempts to appear unperturbed and disdainful in his presence were flimsy screens, hastily erected and easily penetrated, she felt that she was teetering on the edge of an experience that she was ill equipped to handle. Not having traveled to Martinique to become caught in the prickly briar patch of a fruitless love affair, she resented the intrusion into her well-organized life, at the same time admitting that the interplay which had sprung up between them was becoming increasingly intriguing with each encounter.

As she walked up the path to the front door of the cottage, she could smell the pungent odor of a wood fire and saw a thin column of smoke, a wavering plume spiraling against the thick green foliage which almost blotted out the sky.

"An American barbecue tonight," Betsy said as she greeted her, leading her through the living room where Ann and Jeremy were sprawled on the floor absorbed in a game of checkers.

On the brick patio she met David Johnson. Attired in shorts and a casual sport shirt partially concealed by a capacious apron, he was obviously in his element as he carefully tended the fire, pointing with pride to the steaks laid out on a platter. A man in his early thirties, tanned by the tropical sun to a golden brown, he was not handsome. His features were unremarkable, but as with his wife, his informality and high spirits drew Carol to him instantaneously.

Chad Anderson, assigned as his sous-chef, stood beside him, a drink in one hand, a long fork in the other. "I am in charge of turning the steaks and determining who wants them rare, medium or well done," he announced. A short, stockily built young man with a shock of straw-colored hair, he was the opposite of Jules Saint Laurent in appearance and, Carol suspected, equally so in personality.

"Jules called to say he would be late," Betsy Johnson remarked as she came out on the patio with a bucket of ice cubes and a bowl of potato chips.

"Trouble on the sugar plantation?" David asked.

"Something about a machine breaking down at a critical moment."

It was cool on the patio. They relaxed in comfortable chairs sipping gin and tonics from frosted glasses as humming birds darted among the flowers in the garden and the rain forest, close to the cottage, was a reminder that Martinique was and would probably always remain an outpost of civilization, untamed and untouched in its interior by the stamp of modernity.

Candles had been placed on low tables to ward off the encroaching darkness. They were on a second round of drinks when Jules Saint Laurent and Michelle La Roche arrived. The impact of his presence was felt instantaneously, and Carol, drawn to him against her will, wondered what chemistry lay within him which caused his entrance to charge the previously somnolent atmosphere with an unsettling disquiet.

Michelle La Roche, clinging to his arm in a proprietary manner, was a tall, willowy young woman, a cloud of black hair touching her bare shoulders. She was wearing a flame-colored gown which accentuated her supple, voluptuous figure. "I almost refused to come," she said petulantly. "I'm not accustomed to being kept waiting."

"A recalcitrant machine in my factory takes precedence even over you, my dear Michelle." Jules Saint Laurent nodded briefly to Carol as he disengaged himself from

Michelle's grasp and collapsed into the nearest vacant chair. If he recalled the morning's encounter on the beach, he gave no indication. "On days such as this, David, I envy you your nine to five job with time off for a siesta. I understand from Betsy that you and Chad spent the day fishing. How lucky can one be. I was up at sunrise with my rod and reel on the beach and although I didn't have one nibble, I did see a—"

"We were near Diamond Rock," Chad interrupted enthusiastically as Carol thanked him silently for inadvertently checkmating Jules from completing his sentence.

"Rocher du Diamant," Jules murmured, and in the fast-fading light Carol saw the inroads of weariness on his face.

"It sounds romantic," Carol said hurriedly, delighted to see the conversation at least temporarily sidetracked to a safer subject. Flushing, she looked away from Jules, unwilling to give him the satisfaction of noting her discomfort.

"Dangerous would perhaps be a more accurate description," he said dryly. "Shall I bore you with a bit of history? Michelle, I believe, has not heard the story and possibly Chad hasn't, as he's a newcomer too to Martinique."

"I only know," Chad remarked, "that it is treacherous. David warned me today to watch out for the currents. It resembles a great straw haystack, Carol."

"With a siren perched on the top luring sailors to their destruction?" Carol asked with a laugh.

"No sirens," Jules replied, "but back in the early eighteen hundreds during the Napoleonic wars, the British, in order to blockade Martinique, had sailors hoist five cannon to its pinnacle. An impossible task, one would think, but they accomplished it, for some time stopping countless ships from reaching the island with much-needed supplies. Eventually a French squadron captured their position, but it cost them three gunboats and seventy or more wounded men. It was the British who christened it H.M.S. *Diamond Rock*, the only rock to be so honored. I've been told British ships, to this very day, salute it as they pass by. Someday I'll take you there in my sloop if you like."

During the entire recital, he had been staring at Carol unflinchingly as if he were relating the story to her alone.

"Thank you but I'm very busy," she replied hastily, determined not to be enticed by his relaxed mood into a sense of false security. Like Diamond Rock she recognized that he possessed dangerous undercurrents, and she was determined not to be added as another entry on his supposedly lengthy list of conquests.

The steaks were ready, accompanied by a crisp tossed salad and thick slabs of French bread. As they dined by candlelight sipping a full-bodied red wine, Carol grew increasingly conscious that although Jules Saint Laurent did not again address her directly, his eyes were frequently focused upon her, while Michelle La Roche, seated beside him, apparently alert to his mercurial moods, was annoyed.

Replete and lulled by soft night winds into a delightful lassitude, they lingered over their café noir as David played haunting calypso songs on his guitar. Chad smoked his pipe, Jules lit a thin black cigarette, while the moon rose from behind the mountains, patterning the garden. The candles flickered and went out, the moon disappeared behind a bank of clouds and Carol shivered involuntarily when the raucous screech of a bird pierced the stillness surrounding them. To her it seemed that the rain forest was drawing closer, encircling them, making them prisoners.

"It's time to go." Jules Saint Laurent stood up, stretching and pulling Michelle to her feet. "As tomorrow is the Sabbath perhaps all of you would enjoy a visit to my plantation. Sunday is still a working day, but we strike a more leisurely pace."

"Not I," Michelle said airily. "There's communion in the morning and one of Father's tiresome receptions in the afternoon."

"*Pauvre petite,*" Jules murmured. "You do have onerous tasks as your father's hostess." Turning to Carol, he said offhandedly, "And you, Mlle. Spencer, are you also otherwise engaged?"

She hesitated, nettled by his provocative smile challenging her to maneuver her way out of the invitation. Determined to thwart him, she replied coolly, "Not at all. It sounds interesting."

"Until tomorrow then."

They heard the roar of his car as he and Michelle departed. Betsy Johnson chuckled. "He reminds me of Émile de Becque in *South Pacific*. I can't help wondering if he doesn't have a parcel of native children stashed away on his plantation."

"Being French it wouldn't surprise me," Carol said caustically.

"Watch out, Carol," David interposed with a laugh. "I believe Michelle is about to be discarded and knows it."

"That may be, but I don't intend to be her replacement."

Chad Anderson was grinning broadly. "I'm thankful to hear it. Let me drive you home, Carol, and I'll escort you on the grand tour tomorrow if you really intend to go."

"Oh yes, I intend to go. After all he's a neighbor and deserves a minimal amount of courtesy."

He drove slowly along the coastal road to Beau Rivage as if the perfection of the night demanded it be savored bit by bit like a rare wine. "I hope to see you often while I'm in Martinique," he said.

The moonlight outlined his face. She liked what it revealed—an honest young man who, matching his pace with hers, would not cause her heart to beat madly one moment and the next to slow down as she tasted the bitter dregs of frustration.

"I'd like very much to be friends," she said frankly. "Martinique can be a little overwhelming to someone who was born and bred in New England."

Chad Anderson gave her a whimsical glance. "Does Jules Saint Laurent upset that streak of puritanism in your makeup?"

"Does it show? I try to keep it hidden, but I guess I merit the description. Let's say I've built up a strong dislike for men with his carefree attitude towards women. Besides there's more to it than that. He's determined to buy Beau Rivage and sometimes I feel that sooner or later he may outwit me."

They had reached Beau Rivage, wandering together across the terrace to the balustrade.

"I don't see how he could outwit you as long as you are determined not to sell."

"It's nonsensical, I know—a dreary subject."

The moonlight played on the calm waters of the Caribbean, quiescent now in the wake of the storm. A cruise ship, ablaze with lights, glided southward, while an orchestra on board played the Beguine, weaving its plaintive melody into the sound of the waves breaking lazily against the shore.

"It's Carnival time," Chad said. "There'll be dancing in the streets of Fort-de-France tonight. I've been told Ash Wednesday will be the climax. Will you go with me?"

"I'd love to." She flashed him a friendly smile.

They strolled toward the house, dark except for a dim light in the hall. He kissed her gently. Her lips were unresponsive. As she said good night and the heavy carved mahogany door closed behind her, she leaned against it, listening to his footsteps, sharp and staccato on the brick pavement, followed by the sound of his car, heading down the driveway, gradually fading until it could be heard no more.

If it had been Jules with me on the terrace, she thought, he would have said "Let's dance," for such an opportunity to hold me in his arms would never have escaped him. His good-night kiss would have been exciting, not a mere comradely exchange. Annoyed with herself for her obsession with a man whom she had recently declared she disliked, she climbed the stairs to her bedroom, pushing his image firmly to the back of her mind.

Annette had turned back the silken coverlet on the big four-poster bed, placing her nightgown on the pillow with her satin mules carefully lined up on the tile floor. Tired but restless, she moved to the open glass doors, stepping onto the balcony.

The cruise ship had disappeared from view. The beguiling music of the Beguine could no longer be heard, yet the melody lingered in the air. Impatiently she left the balcony and undressing swiftly climbed into bed, but the memory of Jules Saint Laurent persisted, the way he had stared at her across the candlelit table refused to go away, and she wished, before she sought refuge in sleep, that she were attending the last night of Carnival with him instead of Chad Anderson and somewhere in the midst of the merrymaking they would dance to the strains of a calypso band.

CHAPTER 6

It was a day with the sun so dazzling in its intensity that the brilliant landscape of Martinique seemed like a garish painting or a gaudy picture postcard.

Riding in the back seat of the Johnsons' jeep with Chad Anderson beside her, Carol was unprepared for the extent and impressiveness of the Saint Laurents' plantation. As they drove along a dirt road, David Johnson pointed out the cluster of stone dwellings that had once been the slave quarters, which long since abandoned, had fallen into decay. He explained that Martinique had a turbulent history of revolts and insurrections before the system of slavery was finally abolished.

"It was as deeply engrained here on the sugar plantations as it was in the cotton fields of the South," he said. "Now that they have attained their freedom, they are paid wages. Although they have some political clout and some have become well-to-do, economically the white man still wields the power. The class system is and will probably continue to be stratified."

"When did slavery end?" Chad asked.

"Later, much later than in the British Empire. In eighteen sixty, I believe."

"Is Jules Saint Laurent a good employer?" Carol asked. Remembering his overbearing manner, she was wondering if ruling a vast area reminiscent of a feudal estate had caused him to unwittingly transfer his air of possessing unquestioned power from his work to his social life.

"He has the reputation of being both wise and considerate," David replied.

The sun beat down upon them as they drove along. Church bells tolled sweetly in the distance. David drove at a slower pace as they passed groups of men and women with their children on their way to Sunday service—the women dressed in their colorful native costumes, the men more somberly attired in dark suits.

They reached the fields where a group of mulatto men was cutting the sugar cane with machetes while women and youngsters efficiently fashioned the stalks into bundles, balancing them on their heads before loading the trucks, which, when filled, roared off at a rapid rate, leaving a trail of dust behind.

"Here is our host," David said.

He was on horseback, an impressive figure in jodhpurs and a blue shirt stained with perspiration, a straw hat protecting his face from the sun. To Carol he was transformed into an altogether different person from the man who had twice accosted her at Beau Rivage and had sat across from her the night before on the Johnsons' patio.

There was no question that he was in command. He dominated the scene, giving orders to his overseer, but the haughtiness, the disdainful manner of speaking had been replaced by a seriousness, a complete involvement in his work.

Swinging his horse about, he approached the jeep, doffing his wide-brim hat as he suggested they accompany him to the distillery. As he held his prancing horse in check before he cantered down the dusty road, his eyes swept over Carol with the searching, devil-may-care look that never failed to shake her composure.

At the distillery they watched the stalks of sugar cane crushed by iron rollers, the juice running through troughs to huge vats where it was left to ferment. They toured the factory to see the finished product stored in kegs for shipment and the warehouse where the rum in charred barrels was aged for as long as fifteen years before being ready for consumption.

It was close to noon when Jules invited them to the house for refreshments. "My mother is expecting you," he said before riding off.

The plantation house, situated on a shady knoll, was surrounded by formal gardens—a miniature of the grounds of Versailles with marble statuary, stone fountains and sculptured trees and bushes.

"For generations the Saint Laurents were absentee landlords," David remarked as they left the jeep outside the gardens to stroll along a brick pathway that led to the house. "Jules' grandfather was the first member of the family to settle permanently in Martinique. He built Beau Rivage. When his son sold it to your father, Carol, some twenty years ago, this place was built. Nostalgia for France must still have been in his blood."

The house resembled Beau Rivage although it was constructed of stone and was considerably more extensive. It had the same red tile roof, with balconies on the second floor, embellished with delicate ironwork, and colonnades of intricately carved wood.

Mme. Saint Laurent was waiting for them in the salon, a

formal room furnished in the period of Louis XV, the chairs and sofas upholstered in yellow satin.

Her son did not resemble her except for the liquid brown eyes and olive complexion. She was petite and fragile, dressed in somber black, the only relief a string of lustrous pearls. Her snow-white hair, piled in elaborate curls on the top of her head, gave her an air of dignity and elegance.

Acknowledging Betsy Johnson's introduction to Carol Spencer and Chad Anderson, her slender fingers moved among the Limoges china cups placed on a low table before her as she asked whether they preferred coffee or tea.

"Jules will join us shortly," she said, leaning back against the love seat she occupied, focusing her attention on Carol.

"My son tells me you have no intention of selling Beau Rivage." Her voice was low-pitched and musical. "Which doesn't matter in the slightest to me, for I am content here among my possessions in the house my husband designed. But for Jules it has become a cause célèbre. Why he feels so strongly, I have never been able to fathom."

As she spoke Jules entered the room. He had changed into white slacks and a navy blue jacket and was obviously just out of the shower, his black hair slicked back from his forehead, emphasizing the strength of his clean-cut features.

"It should be obvious to you, Mother," he said lightly. "This plantation without Beau Rivage is as crippled as a water fowl with one leg. But let's dwell on less controversial subjects. What did you think of a sugar plantation, Mlle. Spencer? Have you ever visited one before?"

He had accepted a cup of coffee from his mother and sat down gingerly on one of the straight-back gilt chairs, which seemed far too frail to support him.

"I found it fascinating to the point that the next time I

put a lump of sugar in my coffee, I will have added respect
for the work that goes into producing it."

"Well said!" Mme. Saint Laurent bestowed on her a tepid
smile. "Perhaps you have also noticed that as this is a working plantation, our sole concession to the life of leisure is the
house and the gardens, especially the gardens. Although my
husband was born in Martinique, his roots were in France.
We returned there as frequently as we could manage. Have
you by any chance been to Paris, mademoiselle?"

Uneasy that Mme. Saint Laurent was concentrating on
her to the exclusion of the Johnsons and Chad Anderson,
Carol wondered if she had been entirely truthful when she
disclaimed any interest in Beau Rivage or if her invitation to
tea had been carefully planned so that the older woman
could take her measure.

"Regrettably only once. I spent part of my junior year in
college at the Sorbonne and managed to take several trips
through the countryside. Every time I stand on the terrace
of Beau Rivage and look down at Belle Fontaine and the sea,
I think of the Riviera, and a glimpse of your gardens reminded me of Versailles."

"Jules, before they leave you must show Mlle. Spencer
and the others the gardens."

The tone of her voice made it a command rather than a
request. It was obvious that although her son was in control
of the day-by-day operation of the plantation, Mme. Saint
Laurent was the chatelaine of her establishment, and Carol
suspected that she would consider any woman courted by
her son a threat to her authority. Already well versed in
Jules' independent nature, she wondered if he resented her
imperious manner, but decided not as he gazed affection-

ately at his mother and quickly agreed that a tour of the gardens was in order.

The conversation soon revolved around Carnival. "It continues far too long," Mme. Saint Laurent said with a frown. "Ash Wednesday should not be set aside for merrymaking. In France it is the time to do penance, but then we must accept the customs of this island. We cannot make Martinique France, or Fort-de-France Paris."

"Not that you haven't tried, Maman," Jules said teasingly as his mother arose, terminating the discussion by graciously bidding her guests good-bye.

"My mother has taken a liking to you," Jules remarked to Carol. They had finished viewing the gardens and were strolling toward the Johnsons' jeep. He had fallen into step beside her, allowing the others to wander ahead. "Invariably any girl I bring to meet her, she treats courteously but in a rather frigid manner."

"Perhaps it was because she knows I am not one of your girls," Carol replied tartly.

He burst out laughing. "Mlle. Spencer, why is it that whenever we meet the sparks begin to fly?" he asked.

"If they do, you ignite them, M. Saint Laurent."

"Perhaps we could continue our discussion on Ash Wednesday. I have an engagement which I could cancel. It would give me pleasure to be the one to introduce you to Carnival."

"Thank you, M. Saint Laurent, but I too am already engaged. Chad and I are spending the evening in Fort-de-France together."

If he were disappointed, it did not show on his impassive face as he gave her a courtly bow before assisting her into the jeep.

As they drove away, Betsy Johnson said with a laugh, "Beware, Carol, he admires you."

"Is there any girl he doesn't admire?" Carol asked.

As they bounced along the rough road that led to the highway, she only half listened to their conversation as she thought that today she had been given a glimpse into another side of Jules Saint Laurent's complicated personality —the dedicated, serious plantation owner—and it was not the first or the last time that she wished her sojourn in Martinique had not begun with his abrupt and unwelcome entrance into her father's study.

CHAPTER 7

It was close to dusk. The sky was an azure blue. A welcome breeze had sprung up in the bay. It was Ash Wednesday, and the people of Martinique were about to celebrate the final act of Carnival.

Waiting for the parade to begin, Carol and Chad strolled across La Savanne, Fort-de-France's park on the waterfront.

Tall palm trees swayed gently in the offshore wind, surrounding the statue of Empress Josephine, the wife of Napoleon Bonaparte. Attired in her coronation robes, she was looking across the bay to her birthplace, Trois-Îlets, a woman with countless memories, her smile as inscrutable as the Mona Lisa's. In the distance the gleaming white towers of the replica of Sacré-Coeur were outlined in the fading light.

To mark the finale of six weeks of celebration, the colorful native dress had been abandoned, replaced by somber black and white, and as King Carnival was carried in effigy through the streets the haunting strains of the Beguine mingled with the chant of the crowd—*"Valval pas quitté nous,"* "Carnival don't leave us!"

Caught up in the excitement of the moment Carol and Chad watched in fascination as King Carnival was placed on a barge and towed out into the bay, to be set afire with flaming torches.

The ceremony was completed. The blackness of a tropical

night had descended, the stars intensified a thousand times over in the velvety sky, but instead of the crowd dispersing after the demise of their hero, the revelry continued without abatement.

Propelled by the throng away from the waterfront, Chad grasped Carol's hand firmly. Ducking into a side street, he spotted a café with a gay striped awning at its entrance.

"How about an aperitif?" he suggested. Carol gladly consented as he led her to a vacant table on the terrace.

It was pleasant to sit leisurely out of doors, protected by a thick hedge, while they watched the celebration reach a crescendo. There was music and dancing, laughter and the constant murmur of people passing by. Young couples wandered along the street, their arms entwined. Parents, accompanied by their children, were also a part of the informal parade.

Carol half expected to see Jules Saint Laurent in the crowd, but she did not. Probably it's an old story to him, she mused, one that he outgrew with his boyhood. She could well imagine how he must have enjoyed playing Pierrot to some lovely Pierrette, his mask adding a further fillip to the flirtation.

Chad too was engrossed in the flamboyant scene, his expression aloof and slightly condescending. Somehow she could not imagine him engaged in a masquerade, tossing his inhibitions aside as he lost himself in the frolicking spirit of this night. A good anchor to the windward, she thought amusedly. I should feel fortunate he is my companion instead of Jules.

"There's a nightclub not far from here," Chad was saying. "David tells me it's a must if you want to see the Beguine danced as only the Martiniquais can do it. Shall we go?"

"Let's!" She felt wonderfully at ease in his presence, as if he were an acquaintance of long standing instead of someone she had recently met. It was a relief to be free of the unsettling sensations that Jules Saint Laurent had the penchant to evoke. She began to ask him about himself.

"I work for a law firm in New York," he explained. "One of our important clients is a resident of Martinique with some complicated problems to untangle. I was pleased to be assigned to the job—doubly so since meeting you. I planned to be here for two months. I'm tempted now to stretch it out to four or six."

His admiration for her was frank and direct. "Oh, Chad," she said regretfully, "you've selected the wrong woman unless you're willing to opt for companionship. I'm too mixed up at the moment to embark on anything more serious."

"Because of your father?" He paused at a street corner, seriously searching her face.

"Partially. It's no secret—good heavens, it has been written about often enough—that he was a much-married man. It's bound to have made me skittish. Someday I'll probably feel differently. But there's more to it than that. I figure I have a year of freedom to prove whether I can write or not. It isn't very long, but it will have to suffice, for by then my nest egg will be exhausted. It's as if I were walking on a tightrope. Each step is chancy and if I fall it's back to Boston and a nine to five job. I've known too many aspiring writers to be confident that after working eight hours or more a day, one can produce a novel in one's spare time."

"I won't infringe on your writing," he assured her, "but you should play as well as work, and when you play I'd like to be with you."

"Fair enough," she agreed as they reached the nightclub they had been searching for.

It proved to be a *boîte de nuit,* small and intimate. The cabaret was already in progress. The spectators, clustered around tiny tables, were in the shadows, while spotlights under the raised glass dance floor focused on a scene tinged with the flavor of the *Arabian Nights,* the brilliant costumes suggestive of the Orient, the jupes and foulards of the dancers displaying the colors of the rainbow from crimson to blue to green to lilac to rose. With stateliness and infinite grace the women executed the stylized rituals of their island dances, their madras turbans, their elaborate coiffures making them appear much taller than they were. Ropes of jewelry strung around their necks and huge gold earrings, their pendants almost touching their bare shoulders, added to the splendor of the native dress. The cabaret ended with the Beguine. The performers left the floor. Tiny lights, like miniature stars, flashed on in the midnight-blue ceiling as couples left their tables to dance to the strains of a Cuban rhumba.

"Care to join them?" Chad asked.

"Oh, yes, I love to dance."

He proved to be an excellent partner. It was close to twelve o'clock when pleasantly weary they returned to their table. As they sipped their drinks, Carol murmured, "It's been a wonderful evening."

Chad flushed with pleasure. "The beginning of many, I hope. Let's explore Martinique together. I'm looking forward to seeing Mount Pelée when it isn't clouded in mist. My only fear is that I'll not be able to compete with Jules Saint Laurent for your attention."

"Don't worry on that score," she said quickly.

"It's quite obvious he's attracted to you."

"If so, I am one of many others. But in my case, it's Beau Rivage he's after, and I believe I've persuaded him it's a hopeless chase."

They drove back to Beau Rivage in a comfortable silence. His second good-night kiss was as unremarkable as the first. After he had departed, tired but still too stirred by the excitement of Carnival to sleep, she wandered across the terrace for a last look at the sea and the lights of Belle Fontaine, twinkling beneath her in the darkness.

"You were gone one hell of a long time!"

Startled she made out the figure of Jules Saint Laurent leaning against the balustrade. Drawing near she could see him clearly in the moonlight, formally dressed in a white dinner jacket, smoking a cigarette, once more the man-about-town, a stunning contrast to the plantation owner on horseback.

"You're not my keeper," she said crossly.

"That may be true. Nevertheless, I was glad to be here to note that the parting from your escort of the evening was a brief one. *Mon Dieu*, can't Americans show any more emotion than that?"

"I dislike being spied upon," she retorted, her anger mounting with each word he spoke.

"Pardon! It was not my intention to spy. You should be flattered to learn that I left a party, still in progress, to issue you an invitation."

"It's very late. Couldn't you have waited until morning? Besides, as you've probably already guessed, my answer will be no!" Furious that he had broken her quiescent mood, she turned and walked swiftly away from him.

"Carol," he called out. "At least hear my invitation before

you refuse. It comes from my mother, not me. She wishes you to dine with us tomorrow night."

Hesitating, she felt his strong hands grasp her shoulders firmly as he spun her around to face him.

"Why must we always begin with a quarrel and end with one?" he asked in a tone that bordered on the humble.

"I dislike quarreling. The blame for it is yours, not mine."

"If I apologize will you come?" He insisted, "After all, it's unfair to transfer your dislike of me to my mother. She was very much taken with you the other day. She wants to be neighborly."

"If I come, it will be solely because I don't wish to be rude."

"We dine at eight." His smile acknowledged his small triumph.

Tipping her head back as he had done once before, his fingers, like gossamer wings, traced the contours of her delicate features. "You're lovely." His voice had become a whisper, and to her dismay she discovered that she wished to prolong their meeting, that without her volition a spell had been cast, entrapping her as firmly as a fly on a spider's web. Confused, she did not know how much to attribute to his presence or how much to attribute to the allure of the equatorial night.

"You kissed Chad Anderson good night. Am I not entitled to the same?"

"A good-night kiss means very little these days—no more than a casual handshake."

As she made no attempt to escape from the circle of his arms, he drew her closer. "Let's try it then," he said. As his lips found hers, she closed her eyes to blot out the stars which were spinning crazily above them.

"You have no right," she said fiercely.

"No right, but I don't regret it. Do you?"

She did not answer, unwilling to commit herself by words as to how profoundly he had shaken her, her anger toward him replaced by a delicious lassitude, a quixotic desire for him to remain by her side.

His eyes probed deeply into hers. She struggled to look away, knowing she would reveal all too clearly the magnetic force that had drawn her to him from their first meeting.

"Tomorrow night at eight," he repeated.

He did not release her until she said, "Yes, I'll come."

Obviously the victor, he kissed her again, this time a light inconsequential kiss to seal the bargain before he left abruptly in his now-familiar, unorthodox fashion, disappearing into the shadows beyond the moonlit pool.

Appalled that he had effortlessly stormed and weakened her defenses, she felt hot tears of frustration stain her cheeks. To her, passion without love was untenable, and she could find no tenderness in his makeup, no wish to stay the course, but instead a ruthlessness, an overriding determination to dominate, to win.

She searched for the underlying motive that caused him to make her the target of his infatuation. Did he intend to frighten her until she welcomed an escape from Beau Rivage to avoid his troublesome advances? If so, she admitted with a bitter smile, tonight he had unquestionably succeeded in traveling far down the road to reaching his objective.

The waning moon no longer cast pools of warm light on the terrace. Filled with disquiet and unanswered questions, she turned toward Beau Rivage, up until now her refuge, but in her mercurial mood it seemed to have become a pawn in a game whose rules were beyond her comprehension. I may have lost the first round, she thought, her fingers exploring her lips which a short while ago he had claimed, but only the first. She opened the door of Beau Rivage and as she climbed the stairs to the protection of her quiet bedroom, she vowed that tonight would mark his sole victory in what had developed into an implacable contest.

CHAPTER 8

As Carol Spencer approached the gates of the Saint Laurents' plantation, she saw that the house, still some distance away, was awash in lights, crowning the crest of the hill like a brilliant jewel.

Parking her father's Renault at the entrance to the gardens, she caught her breath, enthralled by the flickering torches which lined the brick pathway, spotlighting the marble statuary, the fountains and the beds of spectacular tropical flowers.

Two other cars, a red Fiat and a sleek black Mercedes, were already there. She was thankful not to be the first to arrive. A dark-skinned servant met her at the door, escorting her into the drawing salon where Mme. Saint Laurent and Jules were conversing with their guests. Michelle La Roche stood beside her host, wearing an emerald-green cocktail gown, her black hair a dark cloud around her face. Carol was struck again by her sultry beauty. She was laughing up at Jules, the petulant expression which had been all too evident at the Johnsons' party replaced by an eager, vibrant quality that Carol was certain would be appealing to Jules even if, as David believed, his interest in her was flagging. A handsome couple, she thought, as Mme. Saint Laurent, seeing her approach, smiled and stretched out a hand to greet her.

"You are acquainted with M. Despard, I believe," she

said. Carol nodded to the elderly lawyer with whom she had shared her first evening in Martinique.

"M. La Roche you do not know," Mme. Saint Laurent continued as Carol found her hand being kissed in a courtly manner by a tall, spare gentleman with a narrow, mournful face. "He is our recently arrived *préfet* from France. And Jules, of course, is already your friend, or is he your enemy? I've heard conflicting reports."

"Adversary, Maman, would be more correct," Jules intervened. "Am I exaggerating when I say, Mlle. Spencer, that our meetings have been stimulating although unfortunately, from my point of view, unproductive?"

His dark eyes were examining her closely. It was clear he approved of her appearance. The aquamarine gown she was wearing swirled about her slender ankles, and her skin, lightly tanned from frequent swims in the pool at Beau Rivage, was a pleasing contrast to her golden hair.

"Unproductive in what respect, M. Saint Laurent?" Carol asked flippantly, as soon as she had spoken appalled by the implications her response had engendered, but at the same time pleased that for once she had assumed the role of the challenger.

"Interpret it any way you wish, mademoiselle," he replied with the slow, tantalizing smile that never failed to infuriate her, recalling, to her dismay, the memory of his good-night kiss which had taken place on the terrace of Beau Rivage less than twenty-four hours ago. Blushing she fought desperately to regain her poise and not to act like a foolish schoolgirl who had been overwhelmed by the boldness of her first suitor.

She was saved from further embarrassment when dinner was announced and Mme. Saint Laurent led the procession into the dining salon. She was dressed in black, as she had been the afternoon they met, and Carol wondered if she were in permanent mourning for her husband or if she favored the somber color to accentuate her snow-white hair.

It was a large room with a high ceiling, dimly lit by candles. Dark wooden fans whirred silently above the long table which was covered by an elaborate lace cloth. The glasses and cutlery were of the finest quality. In the center a silver epergne was filled with orchids from Mme. Saint Laurent's gardens, the colors ranging from deep purple to the palest violet.

Mme. Saint Laurent was seated at the head of the table with her son at the foot, extremely handsome in his white jacket and scarlet cummerbund.

"Does Beau Rivage live up to your expectations, Mlle. Spencer?" Jacques Despard was asking her.

"Oh, yes," Carol replied. "I couldn't be happier."

"And your work is progressing well?"

Carol hesitated, always reluctant to discuss her writing, regretting that she had talked so freely to M. Despard regarding her reasons for wanting to remain in Martinique. Finally she answered rather tersely. "It is progressing."

"It's a rare privilege to have a writer in our home," Jules remarked. "Will you tell us, Mlle. Spencer, a little about your work? Are you in the midst of a love story? I hope you are, for Martinique is surely the proper setting for romance. I trust you treat your hero with compassion, not making him a blackguard."

"Love enters into it. However, I certainly wouldn't want to bore you and your guests with the details."

"We would not be bored," Jules assured her.

Aware that they were about to engage in another skirmish

and that the others were diverted by the exchange, Carol was relieved when M. Despard rescued her from her predicament by swiftly changing the subject. "I hear you had an accident on the plantation today, Jules," he said.

"Yes, one of the workers was bitten by a fer-de-lance. Fortunately we have a dispensary on the premises, and he will recover soon."

"A fer-de-lance—what is that, Jules?" Michelle La Roche asked. She was seated on his right, a petulant expression once more on her face, obviously displeased when she was not the center of attention.

"A poisonous snake, my dear," her father intervened. "I've been told it's the only dangerous one on the island."

It was apparent to Carol that M. La Roche had done his homework before accepting his position in this tiny outpost of France. A colorless man, he was the epitome of the well-trained diplomat, always following the correct course at the proper time, handling even the stickiest situation effortlessly and with considerable skill.

"They often hide out in the fields, retreating as the workers cut the cane, but every once in a while we have an accident. No danger as far as you are concerned, Michelle, unless you venture into the rain forests," Jules explained.

"Which I will never do," Michelle declared with a shudder.

"Oh, it's perfectly safe to drive through them. Some day soon I'll take you northward to Mount Pelée. You'll see for yourself how splendid our rain forests are. You too, Mlle. Spencer, would enjoy the trip. Perhaps we should set a date for our excursion." Jules' attention was focused on Carol as he spoke.

"I plan to go. Chad Anderson and I have agreed to be

tourists together, but thank you anyway for the invitation."
Carol smiled sweetly at him, satisfied to note that her answer
displeased him as he returned her smile with a scowl.

"Mount Pelée should be a must on your itinerary, Mademoiselle," Jacques Despard commented. "Although Saint
Pierre has become a small settlement since the eruption, it is
a charming spot to visit."

"I should think that after such a catastrophe Saint Pierre
would be a ghost town," Carol exclaimed. "A city of thirty
thousand people wiped out in a matter of seconds!"

"With one exception," Jules pointed out. "There was a
survivor. Ironically a prisoner who escaped due to the happy
coincidence that the walls of his cell were built of stone."

"On the surface, one would be inclined to agree with your
reaction, Mlle. Spencer," Jacques Despard said. "But you
see, you have failed to take into consideration the fatalism of
our island people. Born and raised under the shadow of
Mount Pelée, they are constantly reminded that life can be
of short duration. Therefore, it should be enjoyed to the hilt,
for the week, the day, the hour. That is one reason why they
dedicate themselves wholeheartedly to Carnival. By observing them closely you will see their deep disquiet and understand why they snap their fingers at fate. How do you say
insouciance in English, Jules?" He turned to his host.

"Devil-may-care, roughly, heedlessness," Jules replied.
"You're right, they do possess such an attitude. Martiniquais
play hard but they are industrious too. I'm very fond of
them, for without their dedication to work, I would have no
plantation. I find them loyal employees despite the fact they
continue to view us transplanted Frenchmen as intruders,
which, of course, we are. They call us *Zoreilles*, not translat-

able into English, but let me assure you far from a complimentary designation."

"The ones I've met have been very polite. The Larousses have become my friends," Carol protested.

"But you're so patently American, my dear," Mme. Saint Laurent interposed with a tolerant smile. "You would never be mistaken for a Frenchwoman. Yet they are invariably as polite to us as they are to you, although the demarcation line is always present. In the last analysis, no race wishes to be conquered, and conquer them we did."

"A long while ago, madame," M. La Roche remarked.

"Time has not healed the wound," Jules explained. "It is there and will always remain beneath the surface."

Carol found the dinner delicious. It was a thoroughly French cuisine spiced with the Creole penchant for introducing exotic herbs into cookery, and as they enjoyed the excellent wines, imported from France, the guests turned to the controversial sport of cock fighting, Jules, to Carol's surprise, thoroughly disapproving, while M. Despard merely sighed and said, "Yes, but it will be with us until doomsday."

Later coffee was served in the drawing room, the men discussing politics and the state of the economy intelligently, revealing to Carol a new side to Jules Saint Laurent, the well-educated man in addition to the serious plantation owner and the sophisticated Frenchman, who had developed the art of flirtation to perfection, and who could not help practicing it whether he was in the midst of analyzing world affairs or on the beach casting his line into the ocean.

At eleven o'clock, she arose and bid Mme. Saint Laurent good night, thanking her for a stimulating evening.

"You are most welcome any time," Mme. Saint Laurent replied graciously.

"I'll drive you to Beau Rivage," Jules said, rising from a love seat where he had been sitting next to Michelle La Roche.

"Thank you but I have my car." Carol was delighted to see that he was disappointed by her refusal.

"You are brave, mademoiselle, to venture forth on your own," Jacques Despard said with a twinkle in his eye.

"It's much safer than a taxi ride," Carol answered with a laugh, recalling her two hair-raising trips from Fort-de-France.

"At least, I will escort you to your car." Jules grasped her arm firmly, making it impossible for her to object without appearing rude.

Outside the torches still burned. Carol walked swiftly along the brick path that led to the parking area.

"It is too lovely a night to hurry," Jules commented reproachfully. "Don't worry, I won't attempt to seduce you. Surely you've noticed that all evening I have put forth a great effort to treat you with the utmost courtesy and respect."

Angered by the taunting tone of his voice, Carol said haughtily, "I considered myself perfectly safe in the presence of your mother and your guests. However, from past experience I have learned that being alone with you becomes an entirely different matter."

They had reached the garden gate. She saw her car was parked only a few feet away.

"Would you believe me," he murmured, "when I tell you that with each meeting I grow more enchanted?"

"No, and I would advise you to center your attention on Mlle. La Roche. She is your type, M. Saint Laurent, not I."

"What makes you think you have learned enough about

me to know my type?" he asked. "Your remark is intriguing but puzzling too. In your extremely well-organized and pragmatic manner, you have placed a label on me, putting me in an unflattering category, I fear, you have decided I am not capable of admiring you."

"M. Saint Laurent"—Carol opened the door of the Renault, slipping behind the wheel impatiently—"I would be a fool on the basis of what I have heard about you and what I have observed to take anything you might say with one grain of seriousness."

"What have you heard about me?" he asked with an amused laugh.

"That you are most unreliable and a girl is wise not to listen to one word you speak."

"Regrettably I must confess I have earned that reputation, but isn't it conceivable you are exaggerating to some degree, aren't all bachelors likely to be tarred by the same brush? Perhaps I have the faculty to become an earnest and constant lover if you'd approach me without so many preconceptions."

"I don't think so, M. Saint Laurent. Any woman who swallowed that line would be a fool, which incidentally I am not."

"You are no fool, a trifle misguided, perhaps. I find you adorable."

She turned on the ignition of the Renault, fearful that the ancient vehicle would fail to start, forcing her to agree to have him drive her home. But after a disturbing silence, it purred contentedly.

"Good night," she called out and as she drove off she was not certain whether to laugh or cry at the curious, unsettling end to the evening.

As she followed the twisting ribbon of the coastal road back to Beau Rivage, she faced the grim, unpalatable conclusion that Jules Saint Laurent had accomplished what no man before him had ever managed to. She was in love with him! How else could she explain the ups and downs of the emotional scale that he could so skillfully play on her heart strings?

She knew that she was merely another challenge to a man committed to wooing and winning any woman who, crossing his path, aroused his amorous nature. He was a Latin through and through, and if she allowed him to continue his pursuit, she feared that in the end, he would have a very good chance to gain his objective. Some women, she admitted, would be willing to take the risk of being discarded with contempt after the first flush of passion was over, but she flinched from such a gamble.

Turning into the driveway of Beau Rivage, she parked the Renault and walked to the balustrade, to the very spot where last night he had made love to her, coming close to possessing her. She was certain he had known how deeply he had shaken her, and she suspected that since then he had become all the more intent on the final victory.

A cool breeze from the sea soothed her cheeks, which were hot and flushed, as she vowed that from now on she would avoid this man who was as dangerous as the fer-de-lance who hid in the cane fields ready to strike the unwary trespasser.

The tranquillity she had searched for in Martinique had become as elusive to capture as a bird in flight, causing her to rail at the vagaries of life that had brought her to this island to a man who could never love her in the only way she considered acceptable.

Martinique, which had beckoned to her—a paradise she had eagerly sought—was now a strange uncharted place, while Beau Rivage was no longer a refuge but a prison from which she was not certain she wanted to escape, even though remaining might change her into a weak petitioner, accepting the crumbs from Jules Saint Laurent's table.

She wondered if she were after all more her father's child than her mother's. If the powerful sexual demands that had driven him from one unfortunate love affair to another had been an intregral part of her from the moment of birth, lying dormant, waiting for Jules, a predator using his enormous charm to demolish the barriers she had erected.

I simply won't see him again, she told herself sternly, looking down on the twinkling lights of Belle Fontaine, which seemed to be asking, Yet can you forget him? while the low murmur of the sea breaking against the rocks below reiterated the same question.

No matter what, I won't leave Beau Rivage, she decided. I'll stay here and fight it out. Why should I relinquish my inheritance because of him?

CHAPTER 9

"Doesn't it ever rain during the day in Martinique?" Carol asked. It was the morning after the Saint Laurents' dinner party and finding herself unable to concentrate on her writing, she had been drawn to the terrace by the laughter of the Johnson children as they splashed about in the pool.

Betsy, stretched out in a deck chair, a floppy straw hat partially concealing her face, answered lazily. "Oh, we have our monsoon season, particularly in the northern part of the island. Some day you'll awaken to a heavy mist that will blot out Belle Fontaine and the sea. Believe me, such a sudden, dramatic change is an eerie sensation."

"Maybe I'll be more productive then. It's difficult to accomplish much in such glorious weather."

"I understand you were hobnobbing with the aristocracy last night. Could that be another reason why you're having trouble concentrating today?"

Carol moved uneasily in her chair, annoyed that Betsy had guessed the real cause of her disquiet.

"Is Jules Saint Laurent the villain?" Betsy continued relentlessly. "I've been in hopes you wouldn't join the ranks of those who find him utterly fascinating although I could hardly blame you if you have. He's so damn attractive that it's lucky for me I'm happily married to David with two lively youngsters to keep me occupied."

"On the contrary, I find him obnoxious." Carol uttered the words with such vehemence that Betsy tipped back her hat and stared at her in surprise. "Come now," she said teasingly, "obnoxious is a mighty strong word. I suppose he's pursuing you?"

"In his own iniquitous way. In return I've been rude to him, in fact downright insulting, but it has no effect on him at all. Why last night he intimated that he was a changed man because of me, that he could become an earnest and constant lover. I wonder how many times he's used that worn-out approach?"

Discarding her determination to conceal her preoccupation with Jules Saint Laurent, Carol suddenly had an overwhelming impulse to discuss him in great detail with Betsy.

"Maybe he was sincere," Betsy said. "After all, there are countless men who after having a few flings turn out to be devoted husbands."

"Jules Saint Laurent a devoted husband? I can't believe it. Why he told me at the outset that he was interested only in an affair, that he never intended to marry."

Betsy smiled. "I remember David saying much the same thing to me once."

"Not David!"

"Yes, David. Do you think I'm naïve enough to believe that he had no peccadillos in the past? On the other hand, I'm certain he was not the Don Juan that Jules appears to be. I wish I could offer some sound and sage advice to you, but I'm not very good at that sort of thing." She paused before adding, "There's Chad Anderson. If you went out with him a lot, Jules might become discouraged."

Carol shook her head firmly. "No, Chad's far too nice to use as a security blanket."

Betsy smiled. "I agree. I'm glad you feel that way. Well, here's my antidote for today. I'm off to the market at Fort-de-France on my weekly shopping spree. Why don't you join me? Later we'll have a leisurely lunch somewhere. Afterwards we could look for an outrageously expensive dress to bolster your morale."

"I'm anxious to visit the market. Lunch is a splendid idea, but visiting the boutiques on Victor Hugo Street would ruin my budget."

"Come on then." Betsy struggled awkwardly to her feet, calling to the children that the swimming hour was over. "We'll drop them off at the house," she said to Carol. "Thank goodness we can afford a maid to give me some relief from child raising, especially now in my delicate condition." She laughed, looking down ruefully at her cumbersome figure.

The marketplace in Fort-de-France was not far from La Savanne, its high roof covering a city block. They strolled through it, Betsy too well acquainted with it to be affected by its unique atmosphere. Carol, on the other hand, found herself enraptured. A native woman glided by, tall, erect, a basket resting on her floppy straw hat. It was filled with pineapples, plump ripe tomatoes and pebble-skinned breadfruit. Although it must have been heavy, she carried it as easily as if it had been a feather, moving gracefully, like the dancers who had performed beneath Carol's hotel window on the night of her arrival in Martinique.

Long trestle tables were piled high with pyramids of vegetables ranging from pale green beans to brown sapodillas and bright red tomatoes. Fruits and flowers too were in abundance, while straw hats and baskets were stacked helter-skelter around the tall wooden pillars. Customers haggled cheerfully over prices. Friends blocked the aisles exchanging greetings, with the crow of roosters adding to the hubbub. It was a scene that would tempt an artist to capture it on canvass.

Carol was fascinated by the sight of an obese elderly lady fast asleep in a sagging chair with four piglets chained to its legs, their loud squeals failing to disrupt her slumber.

"Want to buy one?"

Carol froze at the sound of Jules Saint Laurent's voice. "Wherever I go, you seem to be. Can I never escape from you?" she asked crossly.

"I'm always here on market day along with most of the population of Martinique. You'll soon discover we'll be constantly bumping into one another. I suggest Dominica, the island north of us, if you're in search of privacy. Now about last night—"

"I don't want to talk about last night," she interrupted impatiently.

"But I do. Please, only for a moment to clear up a misconception. You see, Michelle La Roche is not my type at all. I believe that's the expression you used to describe her. Her father and mine were life-long friends. Naturally I've escorted her here and there simply to be polite."

"What is your type, M. Saint Laurent? You've succeeded in arousing my curiosity."

"I'm partial to a blonde with lovely gray eyes, of medium height, smashing in a bikini, but unfortunately possessing a temper that rises to alarming heights whenever I am near her. Will you tell me, Carol Spencer, why we must continue to be adversaries?"

With a shrug of her shoulders, she moved on to a stall where huge slabs of meat were laid out on counters, presided over by butchers in white caps and aprons. Searching for Betsy Johnson, she caught sight of her not too far away, and in her haste to reach her side, she stumbled over a wooden crate. Looking down, she saw that it contained a litter of puppies. She counted five of them, their eyes tightly shut, fast asleep, tiny balls of fur, nestling close to their mother.

"A mixed lot!" Jules said, raising his eyes in mock horror. "Heaven knows who their forebears were—a collie perhaps, certainly an airedale, and I wouldn't be surprised to find a cocker spaniel somewhere on their family tree. An undistinguished lineage, I assure you."

Ignoring his remark, Carol knelt down, gently stroking the smallest one, assuring the alarmed mother that there was no reason to be disturbed.

"Legs too short. Tail too long. He's completely out of proportion, but I'll gladly purchase him for you if you want."

She stood up reluctantly. "No, thanks. I don't need a puppy now to contend with."

"He might ease your loneliness."

"I'm not lonely. Whatever gave you that impression?" Her eyes were blazing.

"Sorry, Carol, but that's how I've judged you. You're fearful of life, fearful of love. Was it your father who made you afraid to face reality or was it some other man?"

"This is not the place for a philosophical discussion." She spoke sharply, relieved to see Betsy hurrying toward them.

"Hello, Jules," she called out cheerily. "Look at these pineapples. They were a real bargain."

Gallantly he took the large shopping basket she was carrying. "It's far too heavy for you," he said. "Where is your car?"

They had left the jeep on a side street, and as they

threaded their way through a tangle of automobiles, bicycles and pedestrians, there was no chance for a further discussion. Carol felt a tug of disappointment when after stowing Betsy's purchases in the rear seat, Jules hurried off with a brief good-bye.

"Like a bad penny," Betsy said with a laugh. "But you must agree he's courteous and terribly handsome."

Carol did not answer as she watched him swing off down the street in the direction of the marketplace, an arresting figure in blue jeans and a white shirt.

"Well, let's have lunch," Betsy suggested. "There's a bistro nearby that specializes in escargot and crepe suzettes that melt in your mouth. Today I'm determined to forget my miserable diet."

They did not mention Jules Saint Laurent again, and as they drove home in the early afternoon, Carol decided that his abrupt departure on the crowded street was a signal that he had grown weary of the chase. She was troubled to discover that this did not bring her any satisfaction.

At Beau Rivage Annette met her in the hallway, greeting her excitedly as she led her to the kitchen. "A present for you, mademoiselle," she exclaimed. "From whom I do not know. It was delivered over an hour ago by an errand boy." She pointed to a basket on a table by the window. Approaching it, Carol recognized the mongrel puppy she had admired a short while ago in the marketplace.

A blue ribbon was tied around his neck with a white envelope attached. She ripped the envelope open and read the message inside.

Introducing Beauregard to you, Mademoiselle Spencer,
in hopes he will make your lonely hours less lonely.

It was signed, Jules.

"The nerve of him," Carol cried out in exasperation. "The man is impossible. I have half a mind to drive over to the Saint Laurents' and drop this puppy on his doorstep."

"But you must admit he is adorable, mademoiselle. Besides it is bad luck to return a gift."

"He is sweet!" Carol lifted the puppy gingerly from the basket. "But too young to be separated from his mother." The puppy began to yelp. "He's homesick," she said, cuddling him in her arms.

"And hungry." Annette filled a bowl with milk. Carol placed Beauregard beside it, but his legs were too wobbly to support him as he collapsed on the floor. Obviously he had no notion of what he was expected to do. They found an eyedropper and Carol painstakingly fed him until finally satisfied, he curled up in his basket and fell asleep.

"Are you going to return him?" Annette asked.

Carol shook her head. "No, I can't be that cruel."

That night the puppy slept in his basket beside her bed. When he awakened, whimpering, she carried him to the kitchen, feeding him again. Later, when she returned him to his basket, he gazed up at her in such a pathetic manner that she knelt down and stroked his soft fur.

"Beauregard," she said wearily, "You are more of a problem than the man who purchased you—a man who accused me this morning of being afraid of life and of love."

Am I afraid? she asked herself. Climbing into the fourposter bed, she lay there in the darkness pondering over her question. She had never thought that she was—wary, perhaps, inclined to be cautious, but not afraid. Admitting reluctantly though that Jules had been right when he had said she was lonely, she regretted that she had rejected his overtures in what, in retrospect, seemed a high-handed fashion.

Drowsily she decided that when next they met, she would be softer, more feminine, not so abrasive. Surely he'll come to see Beauregard, was her last thought before she drifted off to sleep.

CHAPTER 10

The next morning Carol awakened to a world that had been washed by a gentle rain during the night, leaving the air fresh and clean, the waters of the Caribbean a luminous blue. As she stood on the balcony outside her bedroom, she was relieved that she had shrugged off the strange, reflective mood which had plagued her since the arrival of Beauregard.

In fact, today life appeared to be brimming over with promise, to be sampled unstintingly. The gloomy shadows of the night had been replaced by bright sunlight, and she was aware it was due to Jules Saint Laurent's candor when he had spoken to her in the marketplace.

At first, it had been a painful experience to be confronted with such a sharp, perceptive analysis, which had exposed uncomfortable insecurities lurking deep down in her unconscious, bringing them to the surface until she had been forced to admit their existence.

It had been a tortuous route to follow, leaving her drained of energy, yet delightfully relaxed and quiescent, to the point that she was grateful to him for his directness. She smiled, thinking that the gift of the puppy had been a catalyst, and inadvertently Beauregard had become her talisman, the symbol of a newly found freedom, a reminder that life was meant to be lived, not cautiously circumvented.

At last she was eager to take the first tentative steps

toward entering the mainstream of life, instead of avoiding it, but the uncertainty as to how this could be accomplished remained a small, dark cloud on the horizon. Instinctively she knew that Jules Saint Laurent would be involved, and later as she fed the hungry puppy, she speculated as to when she would encounter him again. Anxious to make amends for her intransigent attitude, it became terribly important to see him at once. Knowing she would never summon the courage to make the initial move, she fervently hoped that he would arrive soon to observe firsthand how she was reacting to his unusual present.

After breakfast, she carried Beauregard into her father's study, placing him in his basket by the desk, discovering to her joy that today the words flowed easily, and the paragraph she had struggled over the day before was soon satisfactorily rewritten and revised. It seemed a good omen for the future.

Before luncheon, Chad Anderson called, asking her to accompany him on the promised excursion to Mount Pelée. She refused, using her writing as an excuse, for it had become imperative for her to remain at Beau Rivage, waiting for Jules' expected visit.

Later she swam in the pool and afterward sat in the shade while Beauregard struggled out of his box to explore his new surroundings. It was close to five o'clock when Jules arrived, at the very moment when she had reached the conclusion that he did not intend to renew their stormy relationship.

"Not working?" he asked. Dressed as he had been on the day they first met, in shorts and a casual shirt, he flopped down in a deck chair alongside of her. "I wanted to come earlier but couldn't manage it." His eyes commanded hers and as she turned to greet him, she was lost in their depths, the full impact of his powerful personality striking her like a thunderbolt.

"I'm puppy sitting." She managed to keep her voice carefree and nonchalant. "Beauregard is in need of exercise. I can't risk leaving him for fear he might tumble into the pool."

"I've been told that from birth dogs know how to swim."

"That may be, but I'm not prepared to take the chance. By the way, what a ridiculous name for a dog you poked fun at yesterday."

"Poor unfortunate fellow. He needs stature to make up for his woeful defects. Did you have a restful night or did he disturb your sleep?"

She laughed. "It was not very restful. Beauregard demanded to be fed at frequent intervals. I don't suppose it crossed your mind when you bought him that he's far too young to know what to do with a bowl of milk."

"You surprise me." He was looking at her with amusement. "Walking over here, I was preparing myself for all sorts of recriminations. You're not angry with me because of my gift? I expected torrents of accusations."

"They occurred yesterday when I was tempted to deposit Beauregard on your doorstep. But that was yesterday. Since my nightly vigil, Beauregard and I have reached an understanding. Besides I couldn't take out my venom on a helpless puppy."

"Can I thank Beauregard for bringing us together?"

"Oh, I wouldn't go that far," she protested. "Beauregard shows signs of intelligence, but that doesn't mean he can perform miracles."

"I consider it a miracle we are not quarreling!"

"It's far too lovely a day to quarrel."

"Ah me, can't I claim any credit for your remarkable change in attitude?"

"A trifle perhaps." She glanced at him shyly. His expression was serious and intent, giving her the courage to continue. "I've been thinking over what you said yesterday in the marketplace."

"I've been thinking about it too. I'm regretting that I was so brutally frank."

"Yet you were right, you know. I have been timid of life but not due to another man, as you suggested. I guess my father was the culprit. You can't imagine how difficult it has been to constantly hear him highly praised when people learn that I am his daughter. I used to nod my head and agree that yes, he was a genius, a remarkable man, when I held nothing but contempt for him. Recently, now that I know he never completely forgot me, that in his peculiar way he loved me, my feelings towards him have softened, but because of him, I'm still skittish of emotional entanglements. In fact, as you've probably already guessed, I've never wanted and I've never had any."

As soon as the words were uttered, she regretted them, certain that he would capitalize on her admission, even poke fun at her innocence, her naïveté. But when he answered, his voice was immeasurably gentle.

"Of course I knew. It's written all over you. I am the one to be faulted for my thoughtless treatment. Do you suppose we could begin all over again? Pretend we have just met, if I promise to offer you understanding, if I'm less abrasive, which is one of my less charming characteristics? We could make a bargain. I will act from here on out on my best behavior and you will not act like a frightened maiden who believes she is about to be attacked."

She flushed. "I must have appeared ridiculous."

"I equally so."

"I'd like to be friends. Do you think it's possible?" She avoided looking at him, concentrating on Beauregard and his absurd antics.

His voice was serious when he replied. "We could try, although it's only fair to warn you I spoke the truth when I described you as the type of woman who entrances me. Lord knows I'm no eunuch and surely after the kiss we exchanged on this terrace the other night, you must be aware of the indefinable spark that brings a man and a woman together. It is there or it isn't. It can't be manufactured. It would be dishonest of me to tell you that my interest in you is or will ever be platonic."

His smile disarmed her. His apparent honesty weakened the belief that he was a rascal, a fascinating rascal who, when he discovered a bold approach had been unsuccessful, discarded it for another. Knowing that she was treading on dangerous ground, she found it impossible not to respond to his overtures.

"I want to see you again," she said, "but I can't promise you anything more than companionship."

"Agreed. It's a downright shame, but as it's better than nothing, I'm willing to go along." With a broad grin reminiscent of his former bravado, he shook her hand in an entirely impersonal fashion. "I promise, mademoiselle," he added, "to behave in your presence with admirable restraint and circumspection, not to forget limitless rectitude."

She studied him with growing suspicion. "Now you're poking fun at me."

"Not at all. I'm simply struggling to present the model of

perfection that you so earnestly require. Frankly, I think I've managed it rather well."

Despite herself, she burst out laughing. "I guess I can't expect an instant miracle."

"Well, as we've struck a bargain and sealed it by shaking hands, I suggest we begin this adventure in companionship by driving to Mount Pelée tomorrow. I have business there to accomplish. Suppose I provide the picnic lunch and you ask Mme. Larousse to look after Beauregard."

"All right, until tomorrow then."

"Promptly at eight o'clock."

He left in his usual abrupt manner. She lingered by the pool, relieved that she had possessed the courage to renounce her bondage, yet uncertain about the future with its risks, which without question would always be present whenever she met face to face with Jules Saint Laurent.

Acknowledging that she had fallen in love with him, she doubted if he would be capable of returning her love. Friendship, she knew, would be as elusive for them to capture as a moonbeam playing on the dark waters of the sea. But as she lacked the desire to bid him good-bye, she could only hope that he might discover qualities in her which he had not found in other women, qualities that would become indispensable, drawing him to her forever. It was a vagrant hope, but she clung to it as she chartered a course, unmarked and treacherous.

It astonished her that she was willing to accept the risk of the morass of an affair in order to share his company. He's in my bloodstream, she thought sadly, and if I refuse to test the waters, here and now, love may very well never cross my path again.

Beauregard whimpered—the signal that he was hungry—

and as she scooped him up in her arms, she wished she could peer into the future to glimpse what would occur when she and Jules started out on their journey. She smiled at the futility of such a wish, knowing that what lay ahead was illusory, shrouded in mist like the huge volcanic crater on the crest of Mount Pelée.

CHAPTER 11

By nine o'clock they were on their way northward, the Pitons du Carbet looming ahead, slumbering giants, thickly wooded, sloping toward the promontories that led to the sea. Entering the rain forest, they were soon deep in the jungle. It was cool and quiet there, the mammoth trees covered with lianas, while frail pink orchids broke the long stretches of emerald green.

When she exclaimed over the cassia trees proudly displaying a riot of golden flowers on their branches, he explained that the tree was a symbol of alternating despair and hope, for after the bark peeled, stripping the tree of its dignity, leaving it naked and barren, overnight the blossoms appeared, proclaiming that the tree had not died after all.

"Do I sound like a Michelin guide book?" Jules asked with a laugh. "If so, it's because I am determined to honor the promise I made. Pointing out the sights as we go along seems an eminently safe way to remain on neutral ground."

"As I've never been in a rain forest before, naturally I'm curious."

"Would it be permissible to say," he continued gravely, "that you are particularly ravishing this morning, and am I conceited to suggest that possibly I hold some responsibility for that?"

"You can say it. You have said it, but you can't expect me to give you the credit."

Her pale pink dress, almost the color of the wild orchids in the rain forest, was a pleasing contrast to her light tan, emphasizing the golden lights in her hair, and although she would never admit it to Jules, she was quite certain he was correct and the prospect of a day in his company had given her a special glow that had been previously lacking.

Later he parked the car to one side of the narrow road. Climbing onto the embankment, she gasped at the sight of tier upon tier of tree ferns rising above them to incredible heights, their lacy patterns etched against the sky.

"They make me feel like a pygmy," Carol exclaimed.

"I'm hungry," Jules said as a dilapidated bus, loaded with passengers, rounded a curve, its horn blasting, its occupants in a holiday mood waving at them gaily as they passed by. Retrieving the picnic basket from the trunk of his smart Peugeot sports car, he beckoned for her to follow him.

At first sight, they appeared to be plunging into the thickest part of the rain forest. She held back, remembering stories of the dreaded fer-de-lance, until he called out, "Come on. It's perfectly safe."

They walked along a well-defined footpath to a small clearing where a stream, plunging down from the mountains, had formed a pool before racing onward to the sea. On its sandy bottom, smooth pebbles glistened as if they were coins tossed into a Roman fountain, tokens of wishes made and perhaps granted.

He unfolded a blanket, placing it on the grassy bank, as with a sweep of his hand he said, "Mademoiselle, your luncheon is served."

Sampling the delicious sandwiches, she watched him uncork the wine, wondering how many times he had stopped in this very spot and how many girls had sat beside him listening to the roar of the water cascading into the crystal pool.

"Your favorite picnic place?" she asked him as he handed her a silver cup of cool white wine.

"One of them. I discovered it long ago, and yes, to answer the question in your eyes, I've been here many times, seldom alone."

He was sitting not far away, propped against the slender trunk of a fern tree. The meal completed, he struck a match and lit a cigarette. "You don't smoke?" he asked.

She shook her head, brushing the crumbs from her skirt. The roar of the waterfall, the sweet dank smell of the forest, the weak sunlight filtering through the heavy green foliage, all combined to create a delectable lassitude.

I wonder if he will kiss me? she thought. She was surprised and to her dismay disappointed when he made no move in her direction, remaining stretched out indolently, contentedly smoking his cigarette.

It struck her that she knew very little about him, except that he was a successful sugar plantation owner and that his background was French.

"Where did you obtain your schooling?" she asked, breaking the silence between them.

"Tutors when I was young. Later I was sent to France. I have a degree in engineering from L'École Polytechnique in Paris. It's come in very handy, for as you saw the other day, there's a great deal of machinery on the plantation which has a tiresome habit of breaking down."

"Do you ever return to France?"

"Occasionally, but I have never wanted to remain there for any length of time. Unlike my parents, I am wedded to

the new world, not the old. Martinique is home to me. My
interests lie on my plantation and Beau Rivage."

"So you still want to buy Beau Rivage?"

"I do."

"Yet you haven't mentioned it lately."

"I haven't because you made it clear you had no intention
of changing your mind."

"I can't see why you aren't satisfied with the lovely home
you live in now. Why does Beau Rivage mean so much to
you?"

"It was where I was born and raised until I was ten years
old, when my father was forced to sell. It had been in our
family for generations, and I'm enough of a traditionalist to
feel incomplete without it. When I marry, I should like to
see my children born there."

"You told me once you would never marry."

"Pardon, forgive me, but not precisely. I said I would
never marry you."

"Sorry I don't qualify," she said frostily. "Have you selected the future Mme. Saint Laurent?"

"Don't be angry," he said gently. "You must know by now
how greatly I admire you, but you don't understand the
French. They look at marriage quite differently, you see. For
example my mother favors arranged marriages, believing
they are for the best, especially when they join old established families. She's already chosen the girl. She lives in
Paris, by the way. Not at all pretty, but attractive and intelligent. She'll make a satisfactory wife. I will tolerate her. She
will tolerate any affairs I might care to embark upon. It's the
continental way, and I might add, it has worked out very
well over the years."

"You'll marry soon then?"

"In a year or two." He shrugged his shoulders indifferently. "I'm in no haste. I'm only thirty. There's plenty of time to establish my family."

Carol shivered. "It seems awfully cold-blooded."

"I'm not in the least cold-blooded," he replied with a grin.

"I've already learned that. But somehow I find an arranged marriage distasteful. I could never marry except for—"

"Except for love," he broke in. "That is the stock answer given by an American. You have been brought up under the misapprehension that there are two ingredients to marriage, passion and love, and that they are inseparable. But from the record of divorces in your country, I would say, this has not worked out. One should marry because it is expedient. Both partners should enter into it accepting the fact that it is primarily a business arrangement. If my wife, after she has produced my children, develops outside interests, I will not object. Similarly, she will look in the other direction when I find interests elsewhere. No one is the loser. As I see it, passion is an important ingredient of life. It should be enjoyed to the hilt, while love, at least your definition, is an illusion. It simply does not exist."

From the cold expression on his face, it was clear to Carol that Jules was deadly serious, meaning every word he had spoken. For her it clarified many of his previous actions that had been mystifying. His standards and hers were as opposite as day from night and it would be ridiculous to entertain any notion that she would have the ability to convince him that he was misguided and that such a course would lead, in the end, to bitterness and disillusionment.

"I'm thankful you explained your position with such clarity," she finally replied. "It will serve as my guide in the future. It explains part of your personality that has puzzled me."

"At least you can never say that I have misled you."

"No, I appreciate your frankness although I deplore your beliefs. Somehow I pity your future wife, whose only function will be to provide you with heirs. She would have to be a meek, mealymouthed little creature to accept your terms."

"Which is where you are wrong, completely wrong. French women are as realistic as their menfolk, and I will be spared the company of a nagging wife who will meet me at the door each night demanding an explanation of what I have done or expect to do."

"And the two of you will live happily ever after." Carol could not keep the sarcasm from her voice.

"Exactly, but not being hoodwinked by fairy tales, perhaps a more accurate description would be contentedly."

"Tell me," Carol asked. "If your mother has already selected your bride, won't our meetings disturb her?"

"Not at all. Mother, if it is possible, is even more pragmatic than I. You see, she does not consider you a threat. Naturally, she was curious to meet the new owner of Beau Rivage. It was nothing more than a polite gesture towards a neighbor. She finds Americans entertaining. She considers you charming and doesn't mind in the least that I find you charming too. But enough of this searching analysis." He snuffed out his cigarette. "We should be on our way." He started down the path, adding, "Someday I wager you'll come around to my way of thinking."

"Never," Carol replied forcefully.

Watching him stow the picnic basket in the trunk of his Peugeot, she wondered if he had been completely honest when he had dismissed love with such contempt, if perhaps his explanation had been instead a clever ploy to protect him from forfeiting his independence, making certain that at the outset the ground rules were carefully delineated.

Admitting that she had encouraged him to express his views, she recognized that it was inconsistent to regret that he had outlined them with such frankness. As he turned toward her with a smile that never failed to disarm her, she knew she had reached the crossroads and this was her final opportunity to retreat. Already fully exposed to his ardent nature, it was all too obvious that his scrupulously constructed act of camaraderie would be of short duration. Well, at least I'll enjoy the balance of the day, she told herself, for it will be the last.

Slipping behind the wheel, he tweaked a strand of her long blond hair with a grin. "You're being awfully quiet," he said. "I think I can guess what is going on in that complicated mind of yours. Unsettled by my words, you are vowing never to see me again, while a stubborn little voice inside of you, weak at the moment, is protesting that this should not be the end. I wonder what the outcome of your inward struggle will be? I'm inclined to think the little voice will win."

"No one would ever describe you as modest, Jules Saint Laurent," she said angrily, mortified that he had read her thoughts with such accuracy. "On the contrary, I was feeling sorry for a man with such an unimaginative approach to life. In the end, you, not I, will be the loser."

"An excellent, dramatic statement. You must include it in the novel you are writing. But like a great deal that is said by authors, it is totally inaccurate."

She did not answer, denying his opinion by shaking her head stubbornly as the appalling premonition confronted her that he might be right, that the little voice might very well win out, and having reached the point of no return, it was impossible for her to retreat.

It was early afternoon when they reached Saint Pierre. Jules left her to explore the town while he went off on business. Standing in the village square, she stared at Mount Pelée, which brooded above the limpid waters of the bay and the modest dwellings hugging the shore. Mist clung to its jagged peak like a gray chiffon scarf.

A few ships lay at anchor in the harbor. Shopkeepers were engaged in a brisk business. Housewives paused on the street to gossip. The scene was so tranquil, so ordinary, that it was difficult for Carol to believe that Mount Pelée's volcanic eruption had flung boulders down the mountainside as if they were marbles, while sheets of flame engulfed the town and the harbor became a boiling inferno, capsizing ocean-going vessels as if they were toy ships in a pond.

Jules joined her as she sat on a bench near the waterfront. "These people have courage to live here," she said with a shudder.

"Courage and acumen. The soil is rich due to the deposits of volcanic ash. Someday I'll show you a picture of what it was like before the eruption. Instead of a sleepy village, it was a city with botanical gardens on the mountain and splendid villas overlooking the sea." He gestured to one of the narrow streets that wound its way upward. "Some of the ruins still exist. Perhaps they wish to be reminded that the catastrophe could occur again. Did you visit the museum?"

"No, I thought it would be too depressing."

"Then on to Grand' Rivière," he said.

"Where is that?" she asked.

"At the northern tip of the island. On a clear day like this, you can see the outline of Dominica—the wildest, most desolate of the Windward Islands. If we hurry we'll be able to watch the fishermen returning with their catch. You'll find it an impressive sight."

Grand' Rivière was a tiny settlement hugging a narrow, wind-tossed beach, the sand black from volcanic ash. They arrived as the children were coming home from school and the womenfolk were gathered on the shore to watch the boats, slim, fragile dugouts, their prows knifelike, cut through the heavy surf.

It proved to have been a profitable day. Dolphins weighing as much as thirty-five pounds were unloaded, along with kingfish, redfish and tiny flying fish that had been captured as they spawned on banana leaves floating in the water.

"Jules!" One of the fishermen approached them. "It's been some time since you paid us a visit."

He was a mulatto, his dark face ageless, only his cropped white hair revealing that he was no longer young. His eyes flicked over Carol as Jules made the introduction. "Carol, meet Jean Duclos, the most successful fisherman in Grand' Rivière or anywhere in Martinique for that matter."

"You must share our supper." Jean Duclos was already turning back toward the wooden warehouse on the shore. "Go along, you know the way. My wife will be happy to see you," he called over his shoulder.

"Jean's a very good friend of long standing," Jules explained, grasping Carol's arm and maneuvering her skillfully through the crowd. "Supper at the Duclos' house will be a great experience—that is if you are fond of lobster."

"I adore it. But tell me more about Jean Duclos."

"His grandfather worked on our plantation. He was a slave, but he was granted his freedom. This was done every now and then, particularly by benevolent landowners who found the system of slavery distasteful. A smart, intelligent man, he moved here, making a good living as a fisherman. Jean's father was equally industrious. Jean is relatively well-to-do, although you'd never guess it from his appearance and his home, which is modest."

"He speaks English amazingly well," Carol remarked, thinking of the natives she had met in Fort-de-France, whose patois was impossible to understand.

"Yes, and so do his children. He's insisted that they learn it. Except for his wife, Maria. She's been too busy raising a family. You won't grasp one word she says."

The Duclos' cottage clung halfway up the hillside, indistinguishable from its neighbors, with a neat front yard and a flourishing garden in the rear shaded by banana trees.

Maria Duclos greeted Jules warmly. It was obvious he was a frequent guest as he addressed each of the seven children gravely by name before introducing them to Carol.

The lobster was delectable. Carol, seated at the end of the table with the children, enjoyed listening to their precise, rather stilted English. It was evident they were delighted to have a chance to converse in a language they were eager to master. They talked to her about their school, the games they played afterward and the highpoint of their day when they were permitted to go to the beach and launch their logs, which they had painted in bright colors, paddling beyond the breakers before surfboarding in to shore.

Jules spoke in patois to Maria, who cast shy glances in Carol's direction, causing her to suspect that she was the main subject of their discussion.

After dinner, the oldest boy, Antoine, pulled out a book on geography and when Carol said she was from Boston the children crowded around to see where it was located and to ask innumerable questions. She was deep in the story of the Boston Tea Party when Jules rose and said it was time to leave.

"Stay overnight so Mademoiselle can watch the fishing fleet go out at dawn," Jean urged warmly.

But Jules shook his head regretfully, saying, "Another time perhaps."

He drove swiftly back to Belle Fontaine through the rain forest, now clothed in blackness, the car lights unable to penetrate the thick foliage which edged either side of the road. The occasional huts they had passed on their journey northward were no longer discernible, merged into the darkened landscape, while the scattering of villages far below, clustered close to the shore, were dim patches of light visible one moment, gone the next.

She had never felt closer to him yet at the same time further apart. It was as if there were only the two of them sharing this strange, untamed part of Martinique, and yet for some reason, unknown to her, he had become withdrawn, aloof, deep in a world from which she had been excluded.

Once he commented on how well she had hit it off with the Duclos children, and when she asked him teasingly what he and Maria had been discussing with animation during the dinner hour, he replied brusquely, "You," before lapsing again into silence.

Dismissing his mood as merely another disturbing facet of his extremely complex personality, she began to formulate her closing words to him when they arrived at Beau Rivage. The briefer the better, she concluded. I'll thank him for an enjoyable day, adding that as we are both very busy people with entirely opposing life-styles, it would be wise to say it's been fun but good-bye.

He stopped the Peugeot in the driveway of Beau Rivage and before she could commence her well-prepared farewell speech, he drew her to him roughly, his lips claiming hers with such intensity that her exit lines fragmented and were completely forgotten.

"You promised—" she began breathlessly.

"Having kept my promise all day, surely I am entitled to an innocent good-night kiss."

"Not very innocent," she protested.

"Ah—then you felt the magic too. Tell me, can you think of a more satisfactory way to end our journey?"

The light from the dashboard outlined his strong features and the complacent smile on his face which never failed to infuriate her.

"Your conduct was exemplary up until now," she said, opening the car door and slipping out onto the terrace. "But as you have failed to keep your part of the bargain, I think it would be wise to say good-bye."

"Wise, yes, but dreadfully dull and completely unimaginative. Remember you accused me earlier of lacking in imagination, but you were wrong. Since leaving Grand' Rivière, my thoughts have been taking heady twists and turns, all centered on you, racing ahead to tomorrow and the next day and the one thereafter. It is impossible for us to say good-bye. You, a writer, would certainly never desert your hero and heroine in the middle of a chapter. Well, you can't desert me either. I won't allow it, for I find this exercise in companionship far too challenging."

With a wry twist of his lips, he turned on the engine of his car, calling out to her as he swung around the driveway,

"Tomorrow night at six then. We'll sample the night life at Fort-de-France beginning with dinner at Mme. Sidonie's."

Giving her no opportunity to object, he drove off, and as she hurried toward the welcoming lights of Beau Rivage, she vowed that when he called for her tomorrow, she would have Annette greet him at the door to tell him she was not at home.

Beauregard received her with barks of joy as Annette delivered a detailed report on his behavior, which regrettably had not been exemplary. As she picked him up to scold him for his misconduct, her thoughts wandered to the hours she had spent with Jules, her need to see him again overriding his disquieting definition of love, which had struck a discordant note in an otherwise perfect day. His good-night kiss still burned her lips as her stern resolve to dismiss him from her life crumbled.

"You had a lovely day, mademoiselle," Annette remarked softly. It was not a question, and by her discerning glance Carol knew that she had been unable to conceal her tumultuous emotions and that her struggle to appear cool and composed had been a failure.

"Yes, it was lovely," Carol said dreamily. "Quite wonderful, in fact. We drove through the rain forest and on to Mount Pelée and Grand' Rivière."

"A splendid journey," Annette said gravely.

"It was very splendid, but I'm sleepy after so much good food and fresh air." Stifling a yawn, she turned toward the kitchen door. "Oh, by the way, Annette," she said, making a great effort to sound casual, "I won't be home for dinner tomorrow night."

CHAPTER 12

Mme. Sidonie's establishment was located at Pointe du Bout. They were welcomed warmly and with great ceremony by Mme. Sidonie herself. It was clear by her gesticulations and expressions of delight that she considered Jules Saint Laurent a very special guest.

As they were ushered to a table near the windows, Carol was conscious that their entrance had created a ripple of excitement with the murmur of voices momentarily ceasing as she and Jules became the focus of thinly veiled glances and hushed comments.

Jules, an arresting figure in a white linen suit, paused here and there to acknowledge greetings, while the waitresses, captivating island girls daringly turned out in their colorful native dress, fluttered about him like fragile butterflies.

The bay was spread out beneath them, the lights of ships at anchor scattered like diamonds on the darkening waters. Carol studied the menu with a puzzled frown as tall rum drinks were placed before them.

"You have a wide choice," Jules said with a chuckle. "Does iguana in red wine or stuffed goat shoulder appeal to you?"

She shook her head, looking up from the menu to see that he was staring at her with unabashed admiration. "I'm not that adventuresome," she said.

"But oh, I believe you are. To tell you the truth, I expected the doors of Beau Rivage would be firmly barred when I arrived tonight. What made you change your mind? As I recall when we returned from our jaunt yesterday, you gave me a frigid good-bye."

"That was yesterday," she hedged. "Today I decided a little night life would not be amiss."

"A wise decision." His eyes were twinkling. "Although I admire your dedication to work, an evening enjoying excellent food and wine, followed by music and dancing with a stimulating companion, will probably inspire you to put forth even a greater effort tomorrow. Shall I order for you?"

"Please."

"I recommend the accra—fritters stuffed with fish, lobster, shrimp or crab, whatever you prefer. We'll start off with breadfruit soup and worry about dessert later. And to celebrate our first dining out together, champagne is in order."

She was amused, deciding that undoubtedly Jules was the only man in the world whose voice was provocative when discussing a menu.

"Why," she said with a laugh, "do you always make me feel like a fish that you have caught on your line and are playing with before hauling it in?"

"Sorry. It's a habit I've formed over the years. If a lady appeals to me, as you obviously do, I enjoy immensely the preamble to a love affair, although often I have discovered, to my dismay, that the preamble is more pleasurable than the conclusion. However, let me make haste to assure you that this time that won't be the case."

She flushed, aware that the gown she was wearing was the antithesis of demure and that his eyes were lingering on her bare shoulders and the cleft between her firm young breasts.

She had selected it deliberately, almost defiantly, determined to prove to him that she was no timorous creature hesitant to flaunt her considerable charms. In fact, she had cast all caution to the winds by making a hurried trip into Fort-de-France that afternoon to purchase it—an expensive, diaphanous white chiffon gown, molded to her slender body.

"Sometimes," she said flippantly, "I am inclined to suspect that your reputation as a Don Juan has been exaggerated."

"Don Juan? Who has called me that?"

"Betsy Johnson for one. She warned me from the start to beware of you."

"She was absolutely correct to warn you. However, returning to your earlier remark, it is true I am not quite the rake the Betsy Johnsons of this world consider me to be. I have escorted ladies to dinner, to the theater and even dancing with unparalleled decorum. But you see, once it is bruited about that a man has a flair for acquiring mistresses, it is assumed that every evening on the town is the beginning, the middle or the end of an affair. If what people believed of me were true, I would seldom be out of bed and my plantation would be a shambles. Nevertheless, I have never felt the need to denigrate my prowess. Why should I? Let people believe what they choose to believe."

Carol found she was enjoying the exchange. His words were like the sharp edge of a rapier. It was stimulating to rise to the challenge, to parry each thrust.

She glanced about the dining room. "I must admit," she said, "that whether your reputation is deserved or not, I am on tenterhooks. Too many of your friends or foes have been concentrating on our table, which leads me to the uneasy supposition that I have already been added to your list of indiscretions. Shall I stand up and explain to our audience that our relationship is pristine pure?"

"Not precisely pristine pure if you are including me in your speech. I have already spent several nights with you in my dreams—not, my dear, gazing at the stars and murmuring words of love in your ear."

"As long as possessing me remains in your dreams, I shan't worry."

"But if, as you say, everyone in this room has agreed that we are already lovers, why disappoint them? Why not make their assumption a reality?"

"Sorry—no." Carol hurriedly retreated to safer ground, directing the conversation into such harmless channels as the weather, the delicious meal that had been placed before them and the distinctive bouquet of the champagne he had ordered.

After a leisurely dinner, they left Mme. Sidonie's and strolled toward his car.

"Now for some night life," he said, linking his arm in hers.

"It's too late."

"Nonsense, it's early."

At La Rive Gauche, they listened to the plaintive popular ballads, "Maladie d'Amour" and "Dou-dou Pleure," sung by David Martial with pathos and sensitivity.

To Carol the haunting melodies provided the obbligato to her conflicting moods. She was in love with this man who sat beside her, and her heart told her to surrender to the ecstasy that his presence never failed to evoke—to reach nirvana with him, refusing to consider the consequences. But underlying this main melody, another theme cautioned that such a step would be foolhardy, ending with regret and broken dreams—dreams impossible to repair.

Impatient with this warning voice that made each encounter with him complicated instead of simple, weary of her indecisiveness, she did not protest when later, on the way homeward, he suggested they stop at a nightclub on the outskirts of Fort-de-France.

She was not surprised that he was superb on the dance floor. Her inhibitions melted as she spun like a feather in his arms, tossed this way and that by waves of emotion which up until now had been completely foreign.

It was close to dawn when they drove along the coastal road to Beau Rivage, and as the first streaks of the rising sun penciled the sky, a refreshing wind sprung up cooling her feverish cheeks.

At her door he tilted her head upward. To her surprise, she saw that his lighthearted, chaffing mood had become grave and thoughtful. He made no attempt to embrace her. His reluctance puzzled her.

"Carol," he said softly, "I am not the scoundrel I often appear to be. I want you but on my terms, not yours, and for some fathomless reason I can't make love to you tonight, or tomorrow night or the night thereafter, unless you are absolutely willing to accept my conditions. If you should change, tell me. I'll come running. I'll wait for your call, but if it never comes, I'll understand."

Abruptly he left her.

"Jules," she cried out.

He hesitated, his hand on the door of his Peugeot.

She wanted to run to him, to feel his strong arms holding her close, to tell him not to leave her alone, to assure him she would accept his terms, but instead she said weakly, "I guess then this is good-bye."

"Pay my respects to Beauregard," he replied with a sardonic laugh as he drove off.

She stood there for some time on the terrace, one moment grateful that although he had sensed her capitulation, he had refused to take advantage, the next moment distraught because he had not done so.

Aware that she would never gain the courage to summon him to her, she knew it was too late to retrieve the plateau of peace which Beau Rivage had offered. It had slipped away, destroyed on that afternoon when Jules Saint Laurent had entered and taken stage center in her life.

CHAPTER 13

"It's all over," Carol told Betsy Johnson despondently.

"I'm surprised, after an evening at Mme. Sidonie's, The Rive Gauche and dancing until dawn. It sounds absolutely perfect."

"On the surface it does." Carol had finished her morning dip in the pool and was seated on the edge avoiding Betsy's troubled glance. "I suppose I should be grateful to him for his frankness, although I guessed what his terms would be from the first day we met. There's no doubt he's a buccaneer and like a cat playing with a mouse is confident he will always be the winner. Last night he had a take it or leave it attitude, a 'you call me, it's entirely your decision' approach. It surprised me, for he was astute enough to realize that I had been lulled into a reckless mood by the wine, the music and the setting. I had never been closer to consenting, yet he did not take advantage of the situation." She flushed, already regretful that she had revealed so much of what had occurred in the early hours of the morning.

"I don't know whether to be glad or sorry," Betsy murmured gently. "In your place I would probably have taken the gamble, for it's obvious you love him."

"I do, but I'm not a gambler. He calls me stubborn, but it really isn't stubbornness. It's more an ingrained puritan streak in my nature, in addition to a fear of becoming promiscuous like my father. He and Jules differ in one respect. My father always married the girl although they were basically affairs of short duration. Jules surprised me by leaving the decision up to me, for he must have known I would never muster the courage to make the initial step. Can you imagine me calling him on the telephone and saying, 'I'm yours' or some other ridiculous concession?"

Betsy sighed. "So it has become a deadlock. Maybe it's for the best. I've never seen anyone languish very long for a lost love. That happens only in novels and plays."

They lapsed into silence until Carol, still in a reflective mood, spoke again. "I haven't told you about the afternoon when we drove to Saint Pierre. We stopped to have a picnic on the way. It was a delightful spot, perfect for a romantic interlude, in a clearing on the edge of the rain forest beside one of those crystalline pools with a waterfall tumbling down from the mountains. I fully expected him to make love to me. It was obvious he had selected the place with that in mind. But I needn't have worried. He sat some distance away, smoking a cigarette. He was in a meditative mood and then we had made a bargain to be companions only, a foolish bargain in retrospect."

"Foolish indeed. I can't imagine Jules practicing that for any length of time."

"Well, he did. At least that day he did. He spoke of why he was eager to live at Beau Rivage, startling me when he admitted that some day he wanted to marry and raise his family there."

"I suppose you hoped he was thinking of marrying you."

"Oh, no," Carol answered bitterly. "There has never been any hint of that. To him, love as we understand it is a foolish illusion. It does not exist. It is simply an American misconception, impossible to attain. He was all very cut and dried in his remarks. According to him, he will eventually enter into an arranged marriage. He's even selected his future wife, some girl in Paris of whom his mother approves. I thought at first it might be a smoke screen to discourage any woman who cherished the notion that he was available. Now I believe he was sincere."

"He's thoroughly French," Betsy said thoughtfully. "Many of them still favor such an arrangement. I can see where his mother would approve. She is an aristocrat to her fingertips, inordinately proud of her lineage, and as Jules is her only child, she must yearn to see him established before she dies. Jules, too, must be unwilling to be the last of the Saint Laurents. He'll want a son to carry on the family tradition, which is so important to him. It really would not surprise me if an arranged marriage is exactly what he has in mind."

"But it's terribly cold-blooded, don't you think?"

"To an American, yes, but not to a European." Betsy, who had been stretched out in a deck chair, basking in the sunlight, called to the children that it was time to leave. She started toward her jeep, pausing and turning back impulsively to lay her hand on Carol's shoulder. "Look," she said. "I can't leave you like this. I'll call David at his office and ask him to meet us for dinner at Bakoua. You haven't been there. It's the perfect place to help you forget Jules Saint Laurent. I'll suggest that Chad join us."

"Oh, no," Carol protested. "I've been ducking going out with him. He must be disgusted with me by now."

"Nonsense," Betsy spoke briskly. "He'll jump at the chance. You and I will leave around four o'clock. It will give us time to enjoy the beach and a swim before dinner. I won't take no for an answer."

Not giving Carol the opportunity to decline, she herded the children hurriedly into the jeep, calling out gaily, "See you at four."

With a shrug, Carol conceded that an evening with good friends was undoubtedly the tonic she needed, the first tentative step toward relegating Jules to the past until he became a shadowy figure, no longer capable of playing a major role in her existence.

"Bakoua is mainly for tourists with well-padded bank accounts," Betsy explained. They had left the jeep at La Savanne, not far from the statue of Josephine, and were walking toward a wooden pier that jutted out into the harbor, boarding the ferry already crowded with Martiniquais and tourists. On deck they leaned against the railing as the boat sped swiftly across the water in the direction of Trois-Îlets. It was a brief crossing to a quiet cove where sleek sailing vessels and expensive cabin cruisers lay at anchor.

Bakoua was positioned on the crest of a hill, commanding a splendid view of the bay, reminiscent of those luxury hotels on the Riviera which overlook the Mediterranean. An olympic pool, surrounded with colorful flags of various nationalities, was at one end of the lobby, while terraces, planted with beds of brilliant flowers, descended gradually to the shore, where people were sunning themselves or seeking the shade under blue and pink umbrellas.

"I look like a blimp," Betsy remarked ruefully. They had changed into their bathing suits and finding the sand on the beach so hot that it burned the soles of their bare feet, they sought the refreshing, cool water of the bay. It was crystal clear and they could see their shadows reflected on the bottom as they swam.

Reaching the jetty and shallow water, Betsy cautioned Carol to watch out for the sea urchins clinging to the submerged rocks.

"They resemble harmless puff balls," Carol said with a laugh.

"They may look harmless, but they're nasty little devils. Delicious to eat, but if you step on one you'll feel as if you've been wrestling with a porcupine. A painful experience, believe me I know, for I tangled with some on a coral reef one day. David had to pull the needles out with tweezers."

They sat on the jetty, soaking up the peaceful atmosphere. A sloop far out in the bay anchored, lowering its red sails. A launch, crowded with passengers and covered with a thatched roof, took off from the shore, the sound of calypso music floating to them across the limpid waters.

"Feel better?" Betsy enquired anxiously.

"Much—thanks to you." And it was true, Carol thought. She did feel relaxed and at peace for the first time in many days. Bakoua with its jet-set atmosphere was another world from Beau Rivage, freeing her, at least temporarily, from the spell Jules Saint Laurent had cast.

Later they swam leisurely to the shore, changing into their summer frocks. While they waited for David and Chad to arrive, they ordered tall drinks and sitting on the terrace talked idly of inconsequential things.

To Carol's relief seeing Chad Anderson again did not prove to be difficult. If he had been hurt by her neglect, he failed to show it, and she found herself grateful to Betsy Johnson for pulling her out of the doldrums, as the company of good friends, instead of being onerous, proved to be an antidote.

The dining room open to the windward breezes provided an alluring setting. The food was more American in flavor than Mme. Sidonie's. It could have been a first-rate restaurant in Manhattan except for the music, which was strictly West Indian, the air perfumed with the scent of tropical flowers, and the knowledge that across the bay the lights of Fort-de-France twinkled while above them all Mount Pelée slumbered in the darkness.

The evening was a stunning contrast from the night before with Jules at Mme. Sidonie's. A welcome contrast, Carol reminded herself sternly, acknowledging that she should be thankful to be sitting across the table from a man who would never blatantly attempt to seduce her and whose good-night kiss could only be described as chaste and unremarkable.

Should I marry Chad? she wondered. Surely it wouldn't take much effort on my part to bring him to the threshold of a proposal. He was staring at her now, not bothering to conceal his devotion.

Flustered, she looked away, concentrating on the smartly dressed couples who were languidly circling the dance floor. No, I couldn't do that, she decided. It wouldn't be fair to him. But fair or not, it's far too late to consider marrying a man who lacks the ability to stir me to the least degree. Perhaps if it were not for Jules, if I had remained unaware of the deep emotions he could engender, I could marry Chad, remaining blissfully untouched by crosscurrents of passion, content because I had never discovered their existence.

But because of Jules, she knew it was impossible to regress to a placid plateau, to compromise, to accept mediocrity, for the climb to the great heights of love had isolated her from the uninitiated. Damn Jules, she thought, and was appalled that she had allowed her emotions to carry her onto a storm-tossed sea where she, the victim of its relentless waves, had become a helpless pawn in a losing game.

The conversation was light and inconsequential, causing Carol to wonder if Betsy had warned her husband that the evening must begin and end on a casual note. Losing track of the reason for their laughter, she found herself searching the crowd for Jules Saint Laurent. She would not have been surprised to have caught a glimpse of him seated at a table in the company of Michelle La Roche or some other glamorous creature. But there was no sign of him and she was relieved that he was not there, for even a brief nod or smile would have been enough to unmask her carefully contrived casual mood.

They left before midnight. The drive to Beau Rivage was uneventful as they caromed along the coastal road in the Johnsons' jeep, satiated by the food and the wine, caressed by the warm tropical winds that always gave the tantalizing promise that Martinique, above all else, had been created for lovers.

She unlocked the door of her house, watching the tail lights of the car disappear down the driveway. The Larousses had long since retired to their cottage. The hall was dimly lit, yet she saw a message on the table by the telephone written in Annette's precise handwriting. She picked it up gingerly. Monsieur Saint Laurent called, it said. Dropping it as if it were a hot poker, she heard Beauregard whining in his basket in the kitchen. I suppose he's hungry, she thought, and out of sorts too because I've deserted him for two nights.

Turning on the light, she saw that he was standing on all fours, his tail wagging madly as she approached him.

"You can sleep in my room tonight, Beauregard," she said kneeling beside him, and as she stroked his rumpled fur, she saw the blue ribbon tied around his neck with a white envelope attached. Frowning, she tore it off, staring at her name, scrawled in Jules Saint Laurent's now-familiar dashing handwriting. The message inside was brief.

"I was a fool to leave you last night," he had written. "For once my gentlemanly instincts overcame my desire. In retrospect I realize it was a grave mistake. I want you, Carol. You want me. We're foolish to deny it. Tomorrow I am returning to Grand' Rivière. I can only hope that you will accompany me. Jules."

She dropped the letter on the floor. Mechanically she fed Beauregard before carrying him to her room, where he curled up contentedly in his basket. Undressing, she climbed into bed, wide awake, once more facing the irrefutable fact that no evenings spent with friends, no earnest exchanges with Betsy Johnson regarding her unrequited love affair could assuage the intensity of her feelings for Jules Saint Laurent, for it was all too clear that she had reached a fork in the road with two highways stretching in front of her, one of which she alone must select in her journey through life.

One was a lonely route, broad and straight, leading to solitude and isolation. The other, tortuous, enveloped in mist, hid its final destination. Today she had been certain which she should follow, but since Jules' note, she was once more plagued by indecision.

He wanted her. She wanted him, and he had been honest when he declared her foolish to deny it. "I love you, Jules," she whispered, and as the prospect of never discovering the joy of his arms about her washed over her like a great wave of desolation, she knew her decision had been made and that he had won.

CHAPTER 14

If Jules Saint Laurent had concluded that Carol had raised
the white flag of surrender when she agreed to go to Grand'
Rivière with him, he gave no sign of victory as they drove
northward. They spoke very little, as if the balance between
them was too insubstantial for words which might destroy
the unspoken commitment she had made.

Conscious of his strong, bronzed fingers grasping the
wheel and the chiseled outline of his clear-cut features, she
stole surreptitious glances at him as he concentrated with
singlemindedness on the circuitous road ahead.

It was he who finally broke the silence. "Jean Duclos is
not a wealthy man," he said. "With a flock of children to
educate, I hesitate to visit him empty-handed. I brought
along a ham and wine. The ham will be a treat, for although
seafood is a veritable bonanza to the tourists, it can become
very monotonous as a steady diet."

"That was thoughtful of you," she murmured.

He smiled. "I'm curious to learn why you changed your
mind and came with me today."

"I'm curious to know why you changed your mind and
made Beauregard your emissary," she hedged. "After all, it
was only the night before that you declared very firmly that I
was the one delegated to make the first move. Instead you
did. Why?"

He laughed. "Quite simple, Mlle. Spencer. When I discovered the next morning that I could not dismiss you from my mind, I was appalled, for normally when I am in the cane fields, I concentrate wholeheartedly on my work to the extent that whatever occurred the night before becomes irrelevant. But you kept intervening in a most unsettling manner, and as it was obvious you were far too proud to call me, I had no alternative but to make the first move."

"You're right, of course. I would never have called you," she admitted.

"Yet I was somewhat disheartened to find that my ultimatum had meant so little to you that you were out on the town celebrating."

Carol smiled, unwilling to reveal that it had been an extremely tepid celebration with her thoughts constantly straying to him as she wondered how she could ever adjust to the denouement of their strange, unsettling relationship.

"I admit," he continued, "that my stand the other night was admirable. I simply could not take advantage of a charming girl a trifle besotted by wine, calypso music and dancing. Nevertheless in the stark light of the morning, I regretted that I had been so estimable. Disappointed to learn you were not at home, I felt Beauregard was the perfect go-between to deliver my message. Tell me, I'm intrigued, what does your acceptance mean? Are we still playing the ridiculous roles of jolly companions? I'm not very good at that, you know."

"Let's say I'm curious to see the fishermen of Grand' Rivière launch their boats."

"Nothing more?" He glanced at her and when she did not reply, keeping her eyes directly on the road ahead, he shrugged his shoulders, saying with a laugh, "Perhaps it is better, at least for the time being, not to pursue the matter further. Suffice it to say, whatever the reason, I'm happy you are with me."

As they drove into the rain forest, she felt, as she had the time before, that they were entering an enchanted land, a piece of the world belonging to them alone, and she wished that they would never return to Beau Rivage, but instead could live here forever in one of the thatched huts which, blending into the wild terrain, seemed to offer sanctuary. How foolish I am, she thought. Jules and I will never spend our lives together. This is merely a jaunt, a brief excursion, soon to be forgotten by him. As for me, I am bewildered, unable to determine how I will react when it becomes a part of the past.

It was late afternoon when they reached Grand' Rivière. Jules parked his Peugeot in the narrow lane outside the Duclos' cottage. As they walked up the path to the front door, a neighbor, a stout, bustling matron, called out to them from her yard. "I've been watching for you, M. Saint Laurent. Jean and his family have gone to Fort-de-France. His father has been taken ill. Jean told me to tell you that you are welcome to the use of his house." Arms akimbo, her eyes bright with curiosity, she was staring at Carol, causing her to hesitate and turning to Jules say, "I guess we shouldn't."

"What, retreat because we have no chaperone after we've traveled such a distance?"

"I'm surmising," she said stiffly, "that all along you knew he wasn't here."

Shaking his head firmly, he opened the cottage door and carrying his basket inside, placed it on the trestle table in the kitchen. "Well, let's at least have something to eat before we leave," he said mildly. "Look, here's a note from Jean begging forgiveness for not being present. Will that make you apologize for doubting my integrity?"

He handed her the note. Standing in the center of the small, immaculate kitchen, its stone floor recently scrubbed, with its spotless yellow curtains and brightly polished copper pots and pans creating an aura of warmth and respectability, he was like a small boy asking for forgiveness for some inconsequential misdemeanor. "I've told you before I'm not quite the scoundrel you have imagined," he added.

"Well, I am frightfully hungry," she admitted, "and I suppose there's no harm in having our supper here. Besides—"

"Besides what?" he asked. "Don't tell me you're about to confess that you're glad to be alone with me?"

"I'm glad," she replied in a low, tremulous voice. "Now are you satisfied?"

"Partially." He had found a bucket of wood by the stove. With great efficiency he started a fire. "Knowing Mme. Duclos, I suspect her cupboards are far from bare," he said with a laugh. "While I search for sustenance, why don't you unpack the basket? We'll eat some ham and open a bottle of wine. I'm sure our absent host will forgive us if we raid the pantry."

His competent command of the situation, his occupation with dispelling the chill of the early evening, broke the tension between them, as to Carol it became a lark instead of a dangerous step into the unknown.

His practicality had lessened the turbulent winds of desire which, without the protective presence of the Duclos family, had fanned a flame, causing her to feel like a rudderless ship wallowing in a heavy sea.

He was busy at the old-fashioned stove. "Set the table," he directed crisply. "You'll find cutlery and dishes in the cupboard against the wall."

He had tied one of Mme. Duclos' capacious aprons around his waist, covering his well-tailored suit. His hair was slightly dishevelled, his face flushed from the heat of the fire. He was no longer the impressive plantation owner or the convivial boulevardier. His surprising domesticity disarmed her, and as she lifted the heavy blue and white crockery from the cupboard shelves, she thought that for once in her life she would drift along with the tide. I love him, I am with him. That's all that matters, her soaring spirits told her.

The makeshift meal became ambrosia. They lingered over the wine. He brewed strong coffee before starting a fire in the hearth, for the onset of nightfall had brought a chill into the living room.

She curled up on a couch, sipping the coffee, watching the flames dart upward, as with a sigh of satisfaction he lit a cigarette and leaned against the mantel. "Shall we scurry back to Belle Fontaine?" he asked, his eyes challenging her.

"You have the uncomfortable habit of asking difficult questions."

"Not very difficult. The Duclos have several bedrooms. We don't have to share the same one. Whatever you decide to do, my love, to the world outside your reputation will remain inviolate. The Duclos will never know what, if anything, occurs, and although their inquisitive neighbor will gossip about us tomorrow in the marketplace, her suppositions will travel no further. It's a sort of damned if you do, damned if you don't situation, but as she has already assumed we are lovers, shall we disappoint her?"

Uncertain how to answer, she rose from the couch carry-

ing her coffee cup to the sink. The gush of water from the
faucet spared her the necessity of a reply.

She felt his hands on her shoulders, strong, demanding as
he spun her around to face him squarely. "Shall we disappoint her?" he repeated.

There was no way to evade his kiss. He was holding her far
too securely. Besides she did not want to evade it. The
warmth of his body, the urgency of his lips dispelled the
struggle that had a few moments ago raged inside of her. His
touch and her response to his touch gave him his answer.

"I want you," he murmured.

"I love you," she replied and although he did not echo her
declaration, to her it no longer seemed important, for the
tiny kitchen had become the center of her universe, the only
place to be, and she knew that no matter what the final
outcome of their stormy relationship, she would never forget
this room. It would be stamped indelibly on her mind as
long as she lived—the blue and white china, which she had
placed in the sudsy water, the trestle table with a half bottle
of wine resting upon it and the clock over the mantel in the
living room which was softly chiming the hour of nine.

He led her to a room on the second floor. It was meagerly
furnished with a four-poster bed, with the inevitable netting, one straight chair and a bureau under the dormer
window. It had started to rain, a steady beat against the red
tile roof.

When his lips sought hers, not asking but commanding,
she was possessed by a sensation so foreign that it completely
disarmed her, changing her mood from the wariness of an
animal clearly outlined in the moonlight to a recklessness
and abandon never experienced by her before.

No longer was she in charge of her emotions but instead

eager to succumb to his quest, as with soft movements and whispered words, she urged him to guide her step by step into the intriguing, mysterious world of surrender, a world which now she was committed to explore.

Like a symphony that begins slowly, moving from adagio to allegro to the final, crashing triumphant chords, she was swept along on a tidal wave of desire. At first the strength of his body, the urgency of his demands were such that she feared the latent power within him would shatter her into fragments, but ceasing to resist, she became as pliant as a slender birch tree in the wind, as fluid as a mountain stream moving swiftly to the sea.

Not only did she know that it was impossible to retreat, but she had no desire to retreat, as her fears vanished like night shadows touched by the blinding force of the rising tropical sun.

Aware of her innocence, he guided her tenderly and with rare forbearance to and through the threshold of passion, and it seemed to Carol at the moment they merged and reached fruition that what had occurred between them must be as significant to him as it was to her, that it could not be merely another conquest, soon to become indistinguishable from other conquests. Surely, she thought, he has found this consummation a rare and splendid one, never to be duplicated in the arms of another woman.

Later as they lay quietly, arms still entwined, she felt no remorse, no shame for her surrender, content to sleep, to awake, to savor his lovemaking once more and then to sleep again.

She awoke at dawn. A weak light filtered through the window pane. He had not stirred. She examined his face, vulnerable in slumber, and silently she begged him not to awaken, not to open his eyes, fearful that the hours of ecstasy would be shattered by some ordinary word or gesture, refuting the splendor of the night, reducing it to shoddiness, to the beginning or the end of just another commonplace affair.

Cautiously she slipped out of bed, shivering as the floor was cold against her bare feet. Peering through the window she saw that the rain had ceased, replaced by the first pale streaks of dawn as the lights in the cottages below were turned on one by one while the fishermen made ready for another day at sea.

"Come back to bed," he said.

She started. "We'll miss the launching. The fishermen are already on their way."

"Come back to bed. I'll tell you what will happen."

Slowly she turned, reluctant to face him, fearful of what his eyes might reveal. Would it be triumph, smug self-satisfaction that would be repellent, or worst of all amusement over her lost innocence?

Instead he was smiling an enigmatic smile as he stretched out his hand toward her. She came to him and in his arms buried her head on his shoulder. He held her tenderly as if she were a child in need of consolation. Her cheeks were wet with tears.

"Don't cry," he cautioned. "I can't bear it if you do. Lie still while I tell you what is happening on the beach. I've gone with them so many times. It never varies."

His voice was husky, soothing. "There are forty boats in the fleet. You saw them coming in the other day, slender with prows as sharp as knives. They know exactly when to shove off and when they cut through the breakers, paddling for all they are worth, you're certain they will capsize and be sucked to the bottom of the sea. But, of course, that never happens. They reach calmer waters and raising their home-made sails soon become tiny specks on the horizon until eventually they disappear from view.

"After they are gone, some of the older boys launch their most prized possessions, logs scooped out a little, painted in brilliant colors—red, yellow or blue. The boys are experts too. Beyond the breakers, they point their crafts towards shore, riding in gracefully as if they were on surfboards. It must be great fun, but it's serious too. They are mastering their fathers' trade, for which they were destined from the hour of their birth. We'll watch them another time."

"I'd like that," she said in a muffled voice.

"Feel better?" he asked.

"Much. I've never—"

"I know. Are you hungry?"

"A little."

"So am I, but breakfast can wait. I want to tell you something."

She stiffened. "I disappointed you."

He gave a shout of laughter. "Darling, no. You were marvelous. What I'm trying to say and I'm doing it rather badly is that it was different from other times."

"Was it? I have no comparison."

"You touched me deeply, more deeply than ever before. I'm not talking of the physical part. You're very special."

She sighed. "That's good to know. I'd hate to be just another roll in the hay or a one-night stand, as they often describe it in books. It's gratifying to be special."

He was frowning. "I'm putting it very badly."

"I've never known you to be at a loss for words."

She felt the warmth of his desire and added wickedly, "If

you're hungry, I'll get your breakfast. Isn't that what the woman is supposed to do?"

"You're baiting me and I won't let you get away with it." He pulled her closer. "Come to think of it, although I am hungry, breakfast can wait for quite some time."

CHAPTER 15

Looking around the Duclos' snug, cozy kitchen, Carol felt as if she were a little girl once more, playing at housekeeping. She heard Jules whistling in the shower, which was located just off the kitchen. It was a cold shower, as she very well knew, for she had just completed hers—cold but invigorating.

She searched for a frying pan, found one hanging on a hook above the stove and concentrated on breaking eggs into a large wooden bowl while the iron kettle sang cheerily on the stove.

A housewife without a husband, she thought, frowning, convinced Jules would be less than enchanted by her spurt of domesticity. In fact, she was beginning to feel ill at ease, not at all certain what would be the next step in what she was calling, for lack of a better name, their "relationship." She felt his arms about her as she stirred the eggs vigorously. He was still wet from the shower, a large towel tied around his waist.

"I'll be ready to eat in a moment," he declared, and suddenly it became a beautiful morning after a beautiful night, as she discovered she did not care one rap for what tomorrow might bring.

Settling down at the trestle table and tackling their breakfast with gusto, Jules said, "I've been thinking that I know very little about you, Carol." He paused, laughing. "I mean I know next to nothing about your life before Beau Rivage. It must have been difficult."

"I was a very solemn little girl." Carol bit into a slab of French bread which she had warmed in the oven. "That sounds terrible," she added. "I was never underprivileged. I had lots of love from my mother, but you see, my father always loomed as a large question mark. Why, why had he deserted us? My mother's bitterness towards him was infectious. It was bound to color my childhood. It's only been recently that I have understood that my parents were ill-matched. My father was a genius and a genius is not comfortable to live with, and then my mother's idea of life was diametrically opposed to his. She craved the constant company of people. Afternoon teas and countless dinner parties were her métier, while my father was a loner and the type of friends he cultivated were odd ducks my mother found a bore."

"Yet they were in love at the outset."

"Madly. My mother was a beautiful woman, a southern belle, the type who brings to mind magnolia blossoms and sipping mint juleps on the veranda."

"Which proves my point regarding marrying for love."

"One failure does not prove your point."

"She never remarried?"

"No. She acquired courtly suitors who escorted her here and there. She never grew up really, but in her way she loved me. She saw I had the right clothes and went to the right schools, although I was a disappointment to her. Instead of a debut, I opted for college. I think finding traces of my

father's personality in my nature was difficult for her to
swallow. She died while I was at Smith. After graduation I
went to work in a publishing house in Boston. That's the end
of my story. I trust I haven't been a bore."

"That you could never be." He poured more coffee and lit
a cigarette. "I suppose," he said thoughtfully, "when he left
you Beau Rivage, it compensated somewhat for what you
considered his desertion."

"Yes, it did."

"And your writing? How is that progressing?"

"Rather badly because of you."

"I refuse to be your scapegoat. After all, how can you
write about love until you have experienced it? Surely I have
aided you in that department?"

"Always the egotist," she replied. "I suppose you'll expect
to be the hero in every story I write."

"I'll be dreadfully disappointed if I'm not."

They finished their meal in silence, washing the dishes
and leaving everything exactly as it had been when they
arrived. It is almost as if it had never happened, Carol
thought as they closed the cottage door behind them, for
Jules had become very businesslike, preoccupied with putting the key under the welcome mat and, with a worried
glance at the lowering sky, obviously in a hurry to return to
his plantation.

As they drove back through the rain forest, she was disconcerted by his continued silence, afraid to look ahead to
the fast approaching time when they would reach Beau
Rivage. When we do, what will he say? she wondered. How
does one end or continue an affair? To her it seemed very
awkward. She pictured him giving her a hurried farewell

kiss, saying, "It's been fun, Carol. I enjoyed being in bed with you. When will we repeat the performance?"

With a shudder, she decided that was not his style, that he was far too sophisticated and experienced to end their night together on such a boorish note. Perhaps Beauregard would once more be the go-between, but whatever happened she felt strangely ill at ease.

As they approached Belle Fontaine, the rain clouds that had hovered over them on the journey homeward dispersed, and as the sun burst forth turning the trees into glistening spears of light, it seemed a good omen for the future.

Stopping his car in the driveway of Beau Rivage, he kissed her briefly. To her relief he did not mention Grand' Rivière. Instead he said, "I'll call on you tonight. Will eight o'clock be suitable?"

She nodded her head and he was gone, leaving the empty hours looming ahead of her until they met again. Abstractedly, she greeted Annette. Halfheartedly, she patted the effervescent Beauregard before wandering into her father's study and uncovering his typewriter. An affair is not for me, she decided. I'm not equipped to pay the price, to let him call the tune, setting the time and the place for our meetings and determining when the end should come.

She heard a car in the driveway. Betsy Johnson most probably, she thought with despair. I don't want to see her today. I don't want to see anyone.

Restlessly she moved to the desk, rifling through the pile of typewritten sheets, which was far too scanty, proof that Jules Saint Laurent had not only captured her heart but her ability to concentrate. Startled she looked up as the study door burst open and she saw Jules standing on the threshold as he had done on the afternoon they first met.

"I love you!" he said.

Her eyes widened in surprise. "I thought you didn't believe in love."

"I didn't. At least, I thought I didn't. Now I am slightly perplexed, a trifle frightened but despite my confusion an extremely happy man. Do you think you could put up with me on a permanent basis?"

She had never seen him ill at ease before, and she, too, found herself ill at ease, unable to absorb his startling announcement. "Are you telling me you've fallen in love?" she asked.

"Yes. I suppose it happened the morning we met in the marketplace when Beauregard entered our lives. Although it may have been sooner. I'm not completely certain. I was gun-shy, you see. I refused to admit to myself that I loved you. I tried to disillusion you by my silly definitions of passion and love. When that failed, I stumbled around in a cloud of bewilderment until the night we went to Mme. Sidonie's when I hit upon a solution. I knew you had too much pride to accept my challenge, to call and ask me to return. I thought I had successfully cut you out of my life.

"The next day, when I awoke, I assured myself the crisis had passed, that it was all over. Poor, misguided creature I turned out to be, retracing my steps that very night to leave my note of capitulation in the tender care of Beauregard."

"You mean you want to—" She broke off, still perplexed and puzzled.

"Yes, I do—if you're thinking of marriage. I can't live without you so I suppose there's no other alternative but to become respectable."

She burst out laughing, thinking how like Jules it was to propose in such an unorthodox manner—unorthodox but wonderful. "Oh, Jules, of course, I'll marry you," she cried. "You must have known I would from the beginning."

It was then and only then that he approached her, that he drew her close to him, that his kiss, deep but suppliant, chased the last shadow of doubt from her mind.

CHAPTER 16

As Carol drove along the coastal road to the Saint Laurent plantation on the way to an appointment with Jules' mother, she was thinking of how self-centered lovers were inclined to be, reluctant to admit anyone to their enchanted island, fiercely protective of their territory.

Although she admitted it was childish to be so possessive, to want to bar the gates to all outsiders, she was nevertheless uneasy at the prospect of her meeting with the formidable Mme. Saint Laurent, a meeting which had been scheduled for ten o'clock.

Pushing the fast-approaching confrontation tentatively to the back of her mind, a tender smile played on her lips as she recalled the surprising but marvelous events that had occurred the day before—Jules' astonishing declaration of love in the morning, followed by an evening on the terrace at Beau Rivage where they explored every facet of the wonderful event and discussed seriously what their future would be.

"We'll live at Beau Rivage, of course," Jules had said.

"Of course," she had responded, as for the first time the realization dawned upon her that Jules not only had a plantation to run but a mother who was firmly installed there as chatelaine.

"Have you told your mother our news?" she asked.

"Yes."

"How did she react?" Disturbed by the brevity of his answer, Carol suspected a roadblock ahead of them which would be difficult to circumvent.

He looked slightly embarrassed. "To be honest, at first she wasn't at all happy. I spoke the truth the other day when I told you she was in favor of an arranged marriage, and I agreed with her until I met you. Therefore, it was a bit of a shock, but after a rather stormy session, she gracefully conceded."

How gracefully, Carol wondered wryly, not at all convinced that the stormy session was in the past. "She won't object to our living here?" she asked, shaken at the possibility of living under the same roof with Jules' imperious mother.

"On the contrary, she was relieved. No doubt you've noticed that my mother is the mistress of our plantation house—a role she wouldn't care to relinquish. No, she's happy that we intend to live at Beau Rivage and raise our family here. It's an ideal solution."

It was not until after midnight when he had murmured reluctantly that it was time to leave that he mentioned his mother would be calling her in the morning. "She wants to make arrangements for the engagement party and the wedding," he explained.

"You'll be there?" Carol asked, panic-stricken at the prospect of facing his mother alone.

"Darling, I have a plantation to operate," he had replied. "Besides it will be woman talk, which I detest. I'd be a useless appendage. Knowing mother she is already making lengthy lists. I'll gladly leave the details up to the two of you."

He kissed her then and as he held her close, the meeting

with his mother became inconsequential, something she would face with tranquillity on the morrow, secure in the knowledge that Jules' love for her made any hurdle easy to surmount.

"But I'll be in charge of the honeymoon," he had continued consolingly. "There's a hotel on the Left Bank in Paris that I have in mind, small and intimate. Later, if you like, we'll travel to the Riviera to a villa I know of in Monaco—pink stucco with a splendid view of the sea. We'll dismiss the servants, lock the iron gates behind us and live on love alone."

She had laughed delightedly. "You're besotted," she declared.

"Thoroughly," he replied.

But that had been last night, and now with a feeling that what lay ahead of her might very well be difficult, Carol turned slowly into the entrance of the Saint Laurents' plantation, wishing she had convinced Jules that his presence at this meeting was a necessity.

Mme. Saint Laurent was seated stiff as a ramrod on one of the yellow love seats in the drawing room of the plantation house. Dressed in black, she performed the ritual at the tea table gravely while Carol sat across from her in a straight-backed chair that made it impossible for her to appear at ease.

Feeling not unlike a recalcitrant schoolgirl summoned to the study of the headmistress for a thorough dressing down, she sipped her coffee, waiting for Mme. Saint Laurent to break the heavy silence.

"Jules informs me that he intends to marry you," she said coldly. "It would be unfair not to warn you that although I must concede to his wish, I disapprove."

"We love each other, Mme. Saint Laurent," Carol replied.

"Love!" Mme. Saint Laurent pronounced the word with a shrug of displeasure. "Well, I'll avoid embarking on my rendition of what I believe has occurred. You are aware, I am sure, that I have always favored an arranged marriage, which places me in a most awkward position. In addition, I disapprove of an alliance with an American. Not that I dislike Americans, my dear. In fact, I find them charming, but over the years I have observed that the merging of different cultures, dissimilar backgrounds, is more often than not impossible to accomplish. Jules is a Frenchman through and through, and I very much doubt if you have the least recognition of what that means."

"I'm not concerned over that, neither is Jules," Carol said cheerfully. "Please, Mme. Saint Laurent, do give us your blessing."

"It's a *fait accompli*. What else can I do?" Mme. Saint Laurent spread her delicate hands in a gesture of surrender, smiling faintly for the first time. "I merely felt that you should be informed of my views. Now that you have been, we will proceed with our plans. The engagement must be announced at a formal dinner party. As your parents are no longer living, I expect I am delegated to see it is properly arranged, and as you are a stranger in Martinique, I'll compile the list of guests. In two or three weeks, we should be ready. I visualize a June wedding, or is that too early?"

"Too late, Mother."

With a sigh of relief, Carol saw Jules enter the drawing room, crossing over to her, placing his hands lightly on her shoulders and brushing his lips across her cheek. "Too late," he repeated firmly. "Surely the dinner party can take place very shortly. This is the middle of March and as I am against a lengthy bethrothal, I believe the wedding should be some time early in April. You mustn't be so doctrinaire, Mother."

"As you wish." Mme. Saint Laurent's icy voice registered her dislike of being overruled.

"You agree with me, Carol, that April is the proper time?" Jules asked.

"Oh yes, I agree. And I do appreciate, Mme. Saint Laurent, your willingness to plan the engagement party. It's extremely thoughtful."

"It's the least I can do." Her manner had thawed slightly since Jules arrival, although looking at her patrician, finely drawn features, Carol doubted if she would ever feel comfortable enough in her presence to address her less formally than "madame."

"Well, then that's settled," Jules declared briskly with the typical man's conviction that such affairs as engagement parties and weddings were thankfully outside his sphere of responsibility.

He glanced at his watch. "I'll walk you to your car, Carol," he said, "then back to work for me."

Relieved that the interview was over, Carol thanked his mother for the coffee, and as she and Jules strolled through the garden, she said with a frown, "Your mother is displeased."

"Was she awfully difficult, darling? I sensed it had been rough going when I arrived on the scene."

"She didn't exactly roll out the welcome mat," Carol replied with some asperity. "We skirmished a bit in a lady-like fashion. I succeeded in not losing my temper. I believe the result was a draw."

Jules laughed. "I suppose she gave you the tired old line of the danger of conflicting cultures."

"She did."

"It's a lot of balderdash, don't you think?"

Carol nodded her head in agreement as she opened the door of the Renault.

"Let's have dinner at Mme. Sidonie's tonight," Jules said with a mischievous grin. "This time you can announce to the interested spectators, if you wish, that we are about to be joined in holy wedlock."

"I wouldn't have the courage."

"This might help." Sheepishly he reached in his pocket and pulled out a small velvet box. "I planned to present this to you tonight, but I find I can't wait."

It was a beautiful ring, a family heirloom, a lustrous ruby surrounded by diamonds, and as he slipped it on her finger, her concern over her future mother-in-law's obvious displeasure became relatively unimportant, in fact rather ridiculous.

"Until tonight, darling," he called out as she drove off and she smiled and waved to him, secure once more in the knowledge that no one, not even the dogmatic Mme. Saint Laurent, could disturb the strong bond of love that linked her with Jules forever.

CHAPTER 17

When Carol met Jules that evening at the door of Beau Rivage, he raised his eyebrows in surprise, for she was wearing a simple blue cotton dress. "Not ready for Mme. Sidonie's?" he asked.

"Let's have dinner at home tonight," she said as he slipped his arms around her and tousled her long blond hair. "It's the Larousses' day off and Beauregard will have to be fed."

"Is that the only reason for the change in plans?" He followed her into the kitchen.

She smiled. "You know it's not. I've become quite shameless since Grand' Rivière. I don't want to dine in a public place where I'll have to be dignified and circumspect."

"We've come a long way since the day we first met."

"We certainly have. I'll never forget it. I detested you. You acted as if Beau Rivage were rightfully yours and I was the intruder. I thought you were the most arrogant, impossible man I had ever had the misfortune to encounter."

"I can still be arrogant."

"I prefer the word self-assured."

"And now there's no need for contention since Beau Rivage will be ours."

"Still mine," she replied lightly, "but you may share it with me." Surprised to see that her remark had irritated him, she added quickly, "What's mine is yours, darling, always."

Beauregard's sharp, demanding barks interrupted their discussion, and as Carol fed the hungry puppy, Jules found that Annette had left a kettle of fish chowder on the stove and a crisp salad in the refrigerator.

"It will always be like this," he said. "I'll come home from a day on the plantation, and you'll be here preparing our supper. By the way, can you cook anything more complicated than a scrambled egg?"

"Cooking is not one of my strong points. You'll probably find me in the study, the hour completely forgotten, lost in a romantic love scene while Annette manages the culinary department. Will you mind?"

"Not at all—as long as the love scene in which you are lost is only on paper."

"Silly—I'm a one-man woman."

"And I'm the same only in reverse, but until I met you I wasn't. Carol, do you mind very much?"

She shook her head firmly, placing Beauregard back in his basket. "Not as long as you remain mine for the present and the future."

"Oh, I'm thoroughly yours." He turned off the fish chowder, which was bubbling on the stove. "Shall I demonstrate how thoroughly yours I am?"

"Not now," she protested, protesting no further when he lifted her in his strong arms, carrying her to the master bedroom, which overlooked the terrace and the sea.

His lovemaking was more tempestuous than it had been that night at Grand' Rivière. To her delight she was able to match his passion with hers, her body responding to his with such perfection that her identity became lost as she became a part of him and he a part of her. It was a unity, a harmony that could never be broken.

Not long ago she had considered herself fully integrated, able to exist alone, answerable to the demands of no man, but now incredibly, she had been introduced to what it meant to be fully alive, and as she responded to his caresses like a finely tuned instrument, she looked back with pity to her previous sterile existence.

As they drifted toward sleep, refreshed by a cool evening breeze which stole in from the sea, she asked, "Why is it, Jules, that with me it is different for you than with another woman?"

"Because," he answered lazily. "We've added a new ingredient—love."

Satisfied with his reply, replete, she slept.

"About the engagement party," Jules said. It was later, and they were eating their supper by candlelight in the dining room. "I had a serious talk with Mother after you left, convincing her that this is not a betrothal of royalty and she should scale down her elaborate plans." He grinned at Carol. "Of course, I had a dual purpose. The sooner we announce our engagement, the sooner the wedding will be. Therefore, the dinner party will take place this Friday night. Mother is calling the invited guests on the telephone instead of sending out formal notes."

"Will she include the Johnsons and Chad Anderson?"

"Why don't you ask them? They certainly should be present."

"They are the only people beside you that I really know in Martinique." Carol frowned at the thought of the strangers she would have to meet, wishing that the party could be a small, intimate affair. "You said a dual purpose," she added. "What did you mean by that?"

"I meant that Saturday I leave for Guadeloupe."

"Guadeloupe! Whatever for?" She gave him a puzzled glance.

"Events have piled up too quickly lately. I guess I forgot to tell you about Guadeloupe. I have a plantation there. Not as extensive as this one but very lucrative. Fortunately my manager is reliable and efficient, but every few months I inspect the property. As we're planning an extended wedding trip I feel I must visit it before we start out. It won't be for long, darling, a week at the most. Don't look so downhearted."

"A week seems endless. Must you go?"

"I must. I'd take you with me but don't you think you should be here, finalizing the plans for our wedding?"

"Yes, you're right." Carol managed a smile, impatient with herself for the rush of disappointment at the prospect of seven days without him, seven days with no one to act as a buffer between her and his mother.

"A week will pass quickly. You must have shopping to do and there's your writing," he said, reading her thoughts. "Besides it will be our last separation."

It was midnight when they parted, and as she stood on the terrace watching him drive off, she was unable to shake the alien, disturbing sensation that all that had happened since Grand' Rivière was a dream, a fantastic dream from which she would soon be rudely awakened.

It was foolish, she knew, that to her Jules' trip to Guadeloupe had taken on the proportions of a major catastrophe, but no matter how hard she tried to erase the uneasiness from her mind, it refused to go away, disturbing her tranquillity. Even the memory of his fervent kisses and the engagement ring on her finger, pledging them to each other, failed to diminish the fear that seven days in Martinique without his presence might cause a rift between them.

Jules had pointed out that their courtship had developed with great rapidity, and now faced with his unexpected departure, for the first time she wondered at the metamorphosis which had taken place, changing him from an adversary, to a lover and finally to a man who despite his well-known protestations against a permanent commitment had in a short period of time desired to marry her.

Furious at herself for having the least doubt regarding his sincerity, she concentrated on Friday, the day the announcement of their betrothal would be made, and the all-important question of what she would wear on the evening when she stood by his side and was introduced as his future wife to his many friends.

CHAPTER 18

"I can't believe it," Betsy Johnson exclaimed. "Why only the other day we sat right here on this terrace and you told me it was all over. What happened?"

"It's very simple. We fell in love." Carol responded crisply, finding herself annoyed that Betsy seemed overwhelmed by the news, which served to arouse her own uneasy supposition that perhaps events might have moved too swiftly. "It happens every day," she added firmly.

"But Jules Saint Laurent, of all people, in love. It will send shock waves throughout Martinique."

"Oh, come now, it can't be as earthshaking as all that. I remember you saying, not so long ago, that it was possible his days of philandering were over." Carol frowned, regretting that she had used the word "philandering," for she was convinced now that Jules' reputation had been highly exaggerated.

"Tell me your secret," Betsy said with a chuckle. "You must be a sorceress. We should bottle your talents for future generations."

"Who can fathom what makes a man and a woman fall in love? It must be some strange alchemy between them that they were born with and didn't know existed until *boom*, out of the blue, they meet and it's the Fourth of July and

Carnival rolled into one. To be honest, I don't have the answer."

They were having coffee on the terrace. Carol, dressed in a white linen frock, was on her way to another conference with Mme. Saint Laurent.

"I call it a conference," she explained to Betsy, "because although there are only the two of us present, she's terribly formal. Sometimes I expect her to unearth a gavel from somewhere and strike it sharply on the tea table, declaring, 'Unanimously passed—now on to the next item on the agenda!' You know, I can't help pitying her. She is disappointed in her son's selection of a wife but determined to carry on in a statesmanlike manner. Jules says she has given in gracefully. I suppose in her way she has."

"I wouldn't trust the lady."

"What do you mean?" Carol asked sharply.

"Nothing specific, but don't you think she capitulated a shade too easily?"

"What else can a mother do when a son makes such an important decision? She adores him. She was clever enough to see there wasn't a chance to change his mind. After all, she doesn't want to lose him. We'll get along although I'll never be close to her even if I present her with a dozen grandchildren."

Betsy shook her head. "Nevertheless, you've disrupted her carefully laid plans. I can't see her accepting that with equanimity. Thank heavens you and Jules will be living at Beau Rivage."

"Yes, thank heavens," Carol reiterated fervently. "It's strange, but I was thinking last night that Jules in the end is obtaining his wish to have Beau Rivage. We've traveled full circle since the day we met with love solving the stumbling block between us."

"Probably at first Mme. Saint Laurent believed it was another of Jules' affairs which would peter out before the wedding."

"She did want to delay the ceremony until June, but Jules would have none of it. I fear if that is her hope, she's due for a sad awakening."

Carol watched the Johnson children in the pool, the bright sunlight glistening on their tanned bodies. The rainy spell had been brief and today the cloudless sky promised a perfect setting for the engagement party that evening.

Here at Beau Rivage she knew she and Jules would find peace, adjusting to each other without intervention, and she was grateful that was the case, for despite their strong bond, the prospect of living in the plantation house would have presented a myriad of problems.

Contentedly she watched Beauregard crunching a ham bone which she had filched from the kitchen. Basking in the pleasant scene in a hazy, detached fashion, she thought of the night before, and the night before that, when she and Jules had been together, forced by the advent of dawn to return from the heights of bliss to the ordinary, often frustrating details of everyday existence. He was right, she decided, to insist on an early wedding, for no matter how hard I try to erase disquieting thoughts from my mind, there are forces at work attempting to drive us apart, and despite the warmth of the tropical day, involuntarily she shivered.

"And tonight is the engagement party." Betsy interjected herself into Carol's meanderings, causing her to rise quickly and say, "If I don't hurry, I'll be late."

"I must say I was pleased we were invited," Betsy said with a mischievous grin.

"It wouldn't take place without you."

"Mme. Saint Laurent is noted, you know, for her coolness towards Americans."

"She's told me more than once that she considers us charming. Nevertheless, I made certain that you and David and Chad were on the top of my list. The only ones on my list, to be exact. I'm glad you can come, for the bulk of the guests I've never heard of, much less met. They are mostly French, which means to hear some American voices will be refreshing."

"You'll be married when?"

"As soon as Jules returns from Guadeloupe."

"Guadeloupe! Why is he going to Guadeloupe?"

"Didn't you know? He owns a plantation there. Smaller than this one but apparently profitable. He wants to inspect it before we leave for Paris. We'll be gone six weeks— perhaps longer."

"Paris! How lucky you are. David and I had trouble dredging up enough money for a weekend in Chicago."

"The Riviera too. Jules is renting a villa in Monaco."

"It's terribly romantic," Betsy murmured.

"Sometimes I'm fearful it's too good to be true. What have I ever done to be so fortunate?"

"Nothing's too good for you, my pet. You were due for a break. I couldn't be happier. But tell me, what about your writing? Will there be time in your busy schedule for it?"

"Of course. I'll write better now that I've learned what love is all about." Carol laughed. "I've always had to struggle with romantic episodes, but no longer."

"I suppose all your heroes will be Jules with another name."

"I've already dedicated my first novel to him."

"To Jules, my inspiration," Betsy chuckled. "I believe I'm entitled to the second dedication. After all, I did play a minor role in bringing you two together."

It was all delightful nonsense, Carol thought, as she drove the short distance to the Saint Laurent plantation. Nonsense but great fun to share her happiness with a friend. Dreamily her mind envisioned the future with her and Betsy on the terrace at Beau Rivage, watching her own children splash about in the pool.

In retrospect she could not conceive why she had ever been fearful of falling in love. It was remarkable how swiftly her uncertainties had been laid to rest, that she was no longer bound by her mother's disillusionment and her father's infidelities. No longer an outsider peering through a window on the world, she had become a part of it and she was glad.

Thinking back to the men she had casually dated in college and afterward when she started to work in Boston, she concluded her reluctance had not been wholly due to her parents' sad example, that none of them had been able to awaken her as Jules had done. Perhaps unconsciously she had been waiting for him. If so, she was thankful that she had.

The afternoon spent with Mme. Saint Laurent passed slowly. Dutifully she admired the handsome flower arrangements placed throughout the house. She approved of a receiving line stationed in the entrance hall to greet the guests. She agreed that a calypso band to provide after-dinner dancing was a splendid idea. But as she listened politely to a review of the details which had already been thoroughly discussed several times before, her mind wandered to her wedding day, a ceremony which would terminate the tiresome preliminaries, launching her and Jules on their new life together. Paris in April beckoned to her and yet seemed tantalizingly far away, like a rainbow, ephemeral after a summer shower or a transient moonbeam playing on the dark waters of the Caribbean, while the trip to Guadeloupe loomed ahead like a lowering cloud, an irksome episode barring the way to their escape.

"Just a week, darling," he had assured her when he broke the news of his departure, but a week without him had become a dreary prospect, a wasteland, and she could not prevent herself from toying with the notion that his mother might have been the instigator of his unexpected journey.

Betsy Johnson's candid appraisal of Mme. Saint Laurent's personality, her skepticism regarding her swift surrender, along with the smoothly orchestrated engagement party, all combined to intensify her mood of unreality. It reminded her of a first-class Broadway production, almost too slick, and she, cast as the leading lady, doubted if she could measure up to the critics' expectations.

She was relieved that at least her gown met the specifications. She had spent a frantic afternoon in Fort-de-France searching for it in the smart boutiques, finding it too irresistible to reject as she drew another check on her rapidly dwindling bank account.

It was sea-foam green, the color of the Caribbean on a misty morning, and one glance from Jules as she stood beside him in the receiving line assured her that the extravagant purchase had been well worth it. Even Mme. Saint

Laurent in a rare, confidential exchange whispered to her, "My dear, you are lovely."

The evening proceeded with clocklike precision—the lengthy greeting of guests, the polite congratulations followed by equally polite thank yous, aperitifs served in the drawing salon with an elaborate buffet set up in the dining room and on the terrace. Later there was dancing in the garden where a circular floor had been installed for the occasion.

"I feel like Cinderella," Carol whispered to Jules as they led off the dancing.

"As long as you don't depart at midnight," he said. "It's your introduction to Martinique society, my love. I hope you don't find it too overwhelming. It pleases Mother to launch us properly, but I must admit that despite what you have been led to believe, to me affairs such as this should be presented in small doses, only for very great events. I dislike sharing you with so many people. Tell me, will you be bored at Beau Rivage living with a fellow who wants no one but you as his companion?"

"Need you ask?"

As he held her close to him, under a starlit sky with the flaming torches in the garden holding back the velvety blackness of the night, her answer became totally redundant, replaced by their newly found passion flaring up between them, woven into the sultry music and the fabric of the equatorial night.

It was the only time during the party that she was alone with him, for he was the host, and she, as his fiancée, was called upon to mingle with the guests, repeating over and over again that yes, she and Jules intended to live at Beau

Rivage, and yes, the wedding would be soon, and yes, she couldn't be happier.

Once she danced with David Johnson and once with Chad, who as he whirled her about to the strains of the Beguine, whispered in her ear, "If you ever need me, Carol, I'll be about."

Although she imagined his remark was meant to be friendly, it only served to annoy her, for she suspected her three American friends had agreed that the romance had developed far too swiftly and were already predicting that the dashing, controversial Jules would find it difficult to become a satisfactory, faithful husband.

It was past three o'clock when the last good-byes were said and Jules drove her home to Beau Rivage.

"I leave in a few hours," he said, kissing her as they strolled to the balustrade for a final look at Belle Fontaine and the sea.

"Must you go? I feel desolate already."

"One hundred and sixty-eight hours isn't very long," he told her. "I promise it will be our first and only parting."

Yet despite his saying, "I love you" and the future promise in his searching kiss, when he drove away a cool wind from the Caribbean sent a chill of apprehension through her body, so recently warmed by his caress.

Don't be silly, she lectured herself sternly as she prepared for bed. Certain she would not sleep, she did, awakening refreshed when Annette tapped lightly on her door.

"I brought your breakfast," Annette announced cheerily.

"You're spoiling me, Annette," she protested drowsily.

"It's only right for a young girl to be spoiled when she is soon to be married." Annette smiled as Carol struggled up from the pillows, running her fingers through her tangled hair.

"He's gone to Guadeloupe," Carol said dolefully.

"For a brief time only, mademoiselle. Flowers have already arrived from him to soften the separation, while Mme. Saint Laurent has telephoned twice. She said it was important."

"I expect she wants to discuss the party." Carol yawned, stretching lazily.

"I've heard it was a lovely affair."

"From start to finish." Carol sipped the strong black coffee and toyed with a croissant on her plate. "Now I must get up and see what my future mother-in-law has on her mind," she said.

Dialing the plantation number, Carol listened patiently to a detailed résumé of the night before, with Mme. Saint Laurent casting superlatives over its success.

"My dear," she said when the subject was finally exhausted, "you mustn't forget your appointment with M. Despard at one o'clock."

"What appointment?" Carol asked with a puzzled frown.

"Didn't Jules tell you? How tiresome of him, but still with so much on his mind lately, you'll have to forgive the oversight. Apparently there are a few papers for you to sign. You must realize, my child, that business has an awkward way of encroaching on romance. Monsieur will explain the details, and afterwards do drop by for tea so we can discuss the wedding."

Agreeing that she would drive to the plantation later, Carol severed the connection, picking up Jules' flowers, which were in a long white box on the telephone table. They were red roses, still wet with dew, and as she eagerly opened the note attached, reading the endearing message, she forgot momentarily her bewilderment over her summons to the office of M. Jacques Despard.

CHAPTER 19

"What papers do you have for me to sign, M. Despard?"
Carol asked.

She had been ushered into his private office by a poised,
well-groomed secretary who had closed the door behind her
with grave formality. It was a hot afternoon and a huge fan,
suspended from the ceiling, rustled the papers on Jacques
Despard's intricately carved desk. He was dressed in a white
suit, impeccably turned out. His keen dark eyes gazed at her
benignly.

"It was a superb affair last night," he said, "and you,
mademoiselle, added a great deal to the glamour of the
event. Did you read the report of it in the morning paper?"

"Not yet. I'm sure Mme. Saint Laurent will be pleased."

"Without question. Now for the prenuptial agreement. It
won't take long, I assure you. Signing your name is a mere
formality."

"Jules has never mentioned any agreement to me," she
said with a frown.

"Being thoroughly French I suppose he assumed you
knew there would be matters to settle. It is something that
always occurs at the time of a marriage. He probably forgot
in the hurried pace of recent events to introduce the subject.
Americans are prone to be impetuous when they enter into

an alliance, while Frenchmen insist in spelling it out in black and white."

"May I see the papers, please, M. Despard?" she asked.

"Certainly."

He handed her a document, several pages in length, written in French. She read it slowly, laboriously cutting through the legal verbiage. The first part stated in essence that the Saint Laurent plantation would continue to belong exclusively to Jules Saint Laurent. Carol nodded her head in agreement, for she had no quarrel with that. It had always been and should remain his property.

Further on she saw the name of Beau Rivage and stiffened. Slowly she read the paragraph twice, not believing at first that it stated that at the signing of the document, Beau Rivage would once more become a part of the Saint Laurent plantation. She looked up from the paper, staring at M. Despard in amazement. "I can't believe—" she began.

He interrupted her smoothly. "If you will please sign your name, mademoiselle, on the line I have marked with a cross."

M. Despard lit a cigar and leaning back in his chair gave her a quizzical glance, not concealing his impatience with her careful perusal. "It's very cut and dried. Nothing to cause alarm or raise any dissent."

"Why is Beau Rivage included in this document?" Carol asked, her Yankee shrewdness rising to the surface. "Why in the world should I transfer my property to Jules?" Dropping the document on his desk, she stared at him defiantly.

"Because, of course, he considers it rightfully his."

"If I'm not mistaken this paper states that the moment I sign, Beau Rivage belongs to Jules. Nothing is said about the

transfer taking place at the time of our marriage, and even if
it did, I wouldn't agree."

She saw the cold, calculating look in his penetrating dark
eyes replaced quickly by a bland, unconcerned expression.
Dismayed, she remembered the dinner they had shared on
her first evening in Martinique when he had given her Jules'
offer to buy Beau Rivage and upon her refusal, his warning
that Jules Saint Laurent was the type of man who would
persist, who would never discard his desire to obtain his
objective.

"Jules and I intend to live at Beau Rivage," she said, her
voice unsteady from the shock of her discovery. "Everyone is
aware of that, but the property is mine and will remain
mine. You can file these papers away, M. Despard, for I am
certain when Jules returns from Guadeloupe, he will have a
satisfactory explanation for such a strange request. Until
then, I won't take up any more of your valuable time."

"As you wish." He made no move to usher her to the door
and as she stood up added smoothly, "It would save a great
deal of trouble, mademoiselle, if you would comply."

"Trouble, M. Despard?" she challenged, her anger finally
overcoming her previous composure. "I can see no trouble
between Jules and me. This is obviously a mistake. You must
have failed to comprehend his wishes."

The telephone jangled on his desk. He reached out to
answer and as she turned and jerked open his office door, she
heard him say in a low voice, "Yes, she's here, and yes, there
seems to be a problem."

She drove at a fast pace along the coastal road to Belle
Fontaine, making the hairpin turns with a total disregard of
her safety. If only Jules were here, she kept thinking. I'm
sure then we could straighten all this out. It must be a silly

misunderstanding. Without hesitating, she drove past the entrance to Beau Rivage and on to the plantation, for as Jules was in Guadeloupe, she was in hopes his mother would be able to clarify the miserable situation.

A servant ushered her into the drawing salon, cleared of last night's empty glasses and overflowing ashtrays. It was as if the engagement party had never occurred. She found Mme. Saint Laurent there, her eyes lifting in surprise as without a greeting Carol exclaimed, "Mme. Saint Laurent, what do you know of this document that I am supposed to sign?"

"Do sit down, my dear." Mme. Saint Laurent spoke soothingly. "Whatever has occurred to make you upset?"

"Yes, I'm extremely upset." Carol ignored Mme. Saint Laurent's graceful motion for her to take the love seat opposite her. Instead she remained standing. "Jules has never given me the slightest indication that before our marriage I should sign a prenuptial contract, particularly a contract signing over Beau Rivage to him."

Mme. Saint Laurent shook her head, a sad expression on her face. "Remember I warned you once that the alliance of different cultures usually presents difficulties. I expect Jules assumed you had already guessed that Beau Rivage was part of the bargain."

"Bargain! I don't classify marriage as a bargain."

"Jules does. He always has. Did you expect him to change because he is temporarily entangled in a passionate love affair? Beau Rivage means far more to him than you or anyone else."

"Are you implying that if I had signed the document, he would not have married me?"

"It is possible." Mme. Saint Laurent shrugged her shoulders. "I haven't read the agreement. The wording, of course, is most important. However, I imagine he is prepared to marry you if that is the only way he can obtain his objective. After all, you turned down a handsome offer for the property. What else could he do? You gave him no alternative."

"I don't believe one word of what you are saying," Carol cried out. "Jules and I are in love, there's a world of difference between that and a passionate love affair."

"You are in love, my dear. Yet I must admit Jules is fortunate in one respect. You are lovely to look at and undoubtedly a pleasing companion in bed. It could have been a dismal prospect if the lady in question had been extremely uncooperative and unattractive."

At her words, the memory of Jules' remarks the day of their picnic together flashed in front of her. Hadn't he in essence said the very same thing—that passionate affairs were acceptable as long as one did not believe in a romantic version of love, which was a snare and a delusion. There was no question he had been deadly serious that day. What had ever made her believe that he could suddenly change. She flushed as she remembered how willingly she had allowed him to make love to her at Grand' Rivière, and how smug and self-satisfied she had been when the next morning he had confessed he could not live without her.

She stared at Mme. Saint Laurent, horrified by her words, her complacency, and wondered if she could be in the midst of a nightmare and if she would awaken to find herself in bed at Beau Rivage as the dreadful dream faded, as dreams are inclined to do. But it was not a nightmare, and she was filled with an overwhelming need to leave the Saint Laurents' exquisite plantation house with its expensive furniture and perfectly manicured gardens, to leave and never to return again.

"Good-bye, Mme. Saint Laurent," she said with dignity. It was a miracle she made the return trip to Beau Rivage unscathed, as she saw ahead of her not the narrow circuitous highway but the broken pieces of her first, her only romance.

Shutting herself in her bedroom, she did not emerge until midnight when the house was deserted except for her and Beauregard. Alone she paced the terrace of Beau Rivage, the scene of so many wonderful meetings with Jules Saint Laurent. It was close to dawn before she faced the ugly truth that Jules did not love her and that his skillful campaign to possess her had been a cleverly executed maneuver to deprive her of her property.

Would the marriage have taken place, she wondered, and if it had would she have become simply an attractive appendage, a vehicle to give him the children he desired, a plaything to be discarded when someone more challenging entered his life?

Tearfully she looked about her at the brick terrace, the pool bathed in the waning moonlight, the house plunged in darkness where she had believed she and Jules would live, building a strong foundation on their mutual love. All destroyed, all gone, she thought, a sham, a charade.

Her initial reaction was to defy him, to remain at Beau Rivage in lonely splendor, thwarting him in his Machiavellian scheme to deprive her of her inheritance. But as she thought of the dreary years ahead existing in an environment that would be a constant reminder of the passion they had once shared, she realized that in the last analysis, it would be a Pyrrhic victory. Her vendetta would become a costly triumph as she saw her love for him disintegrate into loneliness and bitterness.

Exhausted she went to bed, but sleep eluded her until she accepted the harsh fact that she must leave Beau Rivage and her broken dreams behind her, that perhaps far away in Boston she would have a chance to gradually forget.

It was noontime when she surprised M. Despard by arriving unannounced in the office, standing before his desk, spelling out her terms in a clear, hard voice.

"I am prepared to sell Beau Rivage to Jules Saint Laurent," she said, "at the price he originally offered. There is one stipulation, however. The Larousses are to remain in their cottage and continue to oversee the premises for as long as they desire. You can put that in writing, M. Despard. I suggest you contact my father's lawyer in New York to iron out the details." Stiffly she handed him a slip of paper with the name and address of her law firm written upon it. He gazed at her in surprise. "Aren't you acting too hastily, mademoiselle?" he asked.

"No, on the contrary, sensibly."

"But wouldn't it be more prudent to wait until Jules returns from Guadeloupe?"

"No, it would only develop into a painful exercise, accomplishing nothing. Jules has made his terms crystal clear. In turn, I have made mine. I assume he will be eager to accept them."

"Oh yes, there's no question but he will accept. He'll take Beau Rivage at any price."

"Naturally. How foolish that I did not understand that from the beginning. Well, I'm not for sale, although Beau Rivage is."

There seemed nothing more to say, so she left him, for she

had reached the end, the finish of her relationship with Jules Saint Laurent the moment she stated her conditions to Jacques Despard. She knew there was only one further step to take, to pack her belongings and bid good-bye to Beau Rivage and the island of Martinique as quickly as possible.

CHAPTER 20

Beauregard, flopping down on the floor beside Carol's bed, had a doleful expression on his face as he watched the frenzied activity surrounding him.

Annette Larousse, removing dresses from the closet and folding them with care, was in tears. "Must you leave, mademoiselle?" she asked. "Even if—"

"Yes, Annette, I must," Carol said woodenly. "But remember you and Étienne are not to worry. As I explained, Beau Rivage will not be sold unless your rights are completely protected." She closed one of her suitcases and with a look of despair at the disorder in the room added, "Some things I will not take, that sea-foam chiffon gown for example."

"But it is exactly right for you," Annette exclaimed.

"Yet it holds distasteful memories," Carol replied, crossing to the window as she heard a car pull into the driveway. "Oh, it's Étienne. I hope he managed to obtain tickets for me on the evening flight to New York." With a gesture of despair, she crossed over to Annette and slipped her arms around her shoulders. "Don't cry," she said softly, "I'm sure M. Saint Laurent will be an understanding employer. Oh yes, one more thing, I'll make certain when I see my lawyer that the Renault goes to your husband. It should be rightfully his, in fact I suspect he is the only one knowledgeable enough to keep it purring on the highway."

Beauregard, as if he felt he were being overlooked in the dispensation of clothes and effects, thumped his tail demandingly on the tile floor. Carol stared at him in dismay. "Whatever shall I do about Beauregard?" she exclaimed.

"Étienne and I will look after him. He's a very affectionate puppy. You can count on us, mademoiselle, to see he will have the best of care."

"No," Carol replied firmly, "Beauregard goes with me. I'll take along one of those wicker picnic baskets to carry him in. He'll be quite comfortable on the plane. Probably the stewardess will think I'm bringing along my lunch, or I'm one of those disorganized females who can never stow all her belongings in her suitcases."

She knew, as she spoke, that it was a foolish decision, but somehow she was unable to sever this last link with Jules Saint Laurent. To excuse her weakness, she told herself that it would be unfair to the puppy to desert him, that it was not his fault he had played such an important role in a romance that had all the earmarks of failure. He'll be a constant reminder to me, she told herself sternly, to never be simple enough to believe what any man says.

Showering, she slipped into the traveling suit she had worn on the day she arrived in Martinique and collected her purse and gloves. Descending the stairs for the last time, she realized that Betsy Johnson knew nothing about the dramatic events of the day that had brought her to the decision to leave. Assuring herself that a letter from the States would have to suffice, she stepped out onto the terrace to climb into the waiting Renault and saw Betsy's battered jeep come speeding down the driveway.

"What on earth is going on?" Betsy exclaimed, gazing in amazement as Étienne loaded luggage into the trunk of the car. "Are you joining Jules in Guadeloupe? If so, it looks as if you're prepared for an extensive visit."

"No, I'm leaving for New York, then on to Boston. I can't explain why, Betsy. I'll write you about it some day. I'm selling Beau Rivage to Jules, and I just can't talk about it. Tell David and Chad good-bye." With a herculean effort she stopped the easy flow of tears and began to laugh helplessly when Beauregard let our sharp barks of protest as Annette lifted him into the picnic basket and firmly fastened the lid.

"Please, don't leave. Whatever has happened, stay with us for a few days. You simply can't take off like this," Betsy begged.

"I can and I will." Climbing into the rear seat of the Renault, Carol signaled for Étienne to start the motor. "It's the only way," she called out to Betsy. "I promise to write, to explain, then you'll agree with me."

Her last view of Beau Rivage was of Annette framed in the doorway wringing her hands on her apron and Betsy Johnson still emitting words of protestation. It's best this way, Carol thought. I can't bear postmortems even with a dear friend.

At the airport, she and Beauregard boarded the evening flight to New York. As the plane flew low over the harbor and she had her last glimpse of Fort-de-France spread out beneath her, awash in the late afternoon sunlight, she said farewell to Jules Saint Laurent and to Beau Rivage, which had at first offered her refuge and in the end would have become her prison if she had remained.

CHAPTER 21

The skies over Boston were storm tossed. A heavy mist hung over the city, drenching the pavements, while a cold wind blowing in from the Atlantic whisked away the last vestiges of winter. It was a typical, mercurial April day, but after the brilliant sunlight of Martinique it was a depressing sight, and it matched Carol's somber mood.

She had stopped in New York only long enough to contact her father's lawyer with the news that Beau Rivage would soon be sold. He received her instructions in his usual non-committal manner, pointing out, however, that $300,000 was a bargain for the purchaser.

"Property in Martinique is rapidly increasing in value," he explained. "You might very well be able to obtain a higher price."

"An offer has already been made," she informed him impatiently, speaking from a telephone booth at Kennedy. "As far as I am concerned, the quicker it is sold the better. I'm satisfied with the price. Therefore when a M. Jacques Despard contacts you, please finalize the sale as soon as possible. I'll write further details from Boston, giving you my new address."

As she hung up, barely catching her connecting flight, it seemed years, not weeks, since she had sublet her apartment to Ann Sinclair, a college friend. I'll only impose on her for a few days, she thought, hoping that her sudden unannounced appearance, accompanied by a puppy, would not present too great a problem.

"Of course you can stay here," Ann Sinclair spoke warmly as she greeted Carol at the door of the walk-up flat. "The dog too for that matter. But tell me, why have you left Martinique? From the letter I received the other day you sounded as if you had found the end of the rainbow there and intended to remain forever."   ·

"It was the end all right." Carol spoke with such bitterness that Ann shifted to another subject. "I wouldn't be surprised if you could get your old job back, if you want it," she said briskly. "I met your boss, Charles Caldwell, at a cocktail party recently. It's obvious they miss you."

It was Sunday. Carol dropped her suitcases in the center of the living room, looking around her. After Beau Rivage with its expansive, airy rooms, the apartment seemed cramped and unattractive. Even the plants in hanging baskets at the windows appeared wilted and neglected.

"I'll sleep on the couch," Carol said. "You'll find Beauregard most cooperative as long as he is with me."

Ann laughed as Beauregard hopped out of the picnic basket, stretching before touring the apartment leisurely. "He's a strange-looking animal," she remarked.

"Strange but lovable and extremely intelligent. I hadn't the heart to leave him behind."

Beauregard barked as if in agreement, appearing from the bedroom with a slipper in his mouth. "He has a penchant for chewing leather," Carol said, bending down to retrieve the stolen object. "But don't worry, just put things that you treasure in closets or on shelves he's too tiny to reach."

Over coffee and sandwiches, they carefully skirted the

subject of Martinique. Ann, quick to sense her friend's unhappiness, avoided the obvious questions, overcoming her natural curiosity to discover what had caused Carol's unexpected return from a journey which began with such high hopes, promising to be of long if not permanent duration.

"Your novel, how is that progressing?" she asked.

Carol winced. "Slowly, only four chapters completed."

"Enough to submit to your publishing house for consideration?"

"I've been considering that." With difficulty, Carol shut out the haunting memories of Martinique, doubtful if there would ever be a time when they would not bob up to the surface, disturbing her equilibrium. "I still have a pittance in the bank, and if I were lucky enough to obtain an advance, I could eke out an existence until it's completed. Tomorrow I'll start knocking on doors."

She spent a miserable night on the narrow, lumpy couch in the living room, with Beauregard stretched out on the floor, sleeping peacefully, remarkably undisturbed by the dramatic change in his life-style.

Tossing and turning until dawn, she could not erase from her mind the shock of the prenuptial agreement and the cruel words spoken by Mme. Saint Laurent as they faced one another in the drawing salon of the plantation house. Perhaps I was too hasty. Perhaps I should have waited for Jules' return from Guadeloupe, she thought, only to reject the idea out of hand, knowing that without question he would have attempted and very likely succeeded in destroying every objection she raised with words of love, words to which she, in the end, would have succumbed as he trapped her in the morass of passion until she had forfeited her rights to an equal partnership, taking the first step toward becoming his slave.

In the morning, with a bright blue sky above and a hint of spring in the air, the shadows that had prevented sleep during the night disappeared as Carol, dressing with care in a blue tweed suit, rode with Ann on the subway to the heart of the Boston business district.

"Good luck," Ann said jauntily as they parted at the street corner where her old office was located, Ann heading toward her day's work with an insurance company, while Carol, her manuscript in her briefcase, warily approached the place where she had been employed.

Charles Caldwell greeted her warmly. "Back so soon," he said, as if she had taken a coffee break instead of a trip to Martinique. "Your old job is waiting for you if you want it."

His eyes wandered to the briefcase she held on her lap. "Don't tell me you've finished your novel that quickly."

"Only four chapters," Carol admitted ruefully.

"And you want me to read what you've accomplished. Well, I will."

"Could you give me an answer soon?" she asked anxiously. "For if you like it enough, if you consider it has possibilities, I still have some money in the bank, and I'd gamble on it to support me until the novel's completed."

"It's a bargain," he replied.

She winced at the word "bargain."

"What's wrong, Carol Spencer?" he asked gently, an astute, kindly middle-aged man who had always treated her as an equal rather than a girl fresh out of college, inexperienced in the literary world. His solicitude shattered her grim determination to remain cool and professional from the start to the finish of their interview.

"An unhappy love affair?" he asked.

Mutely she nodded her head in agreement.

"I suppose it seems the end of the world to you?"

She nodded her head again, fearful if she uttered one word, she would embarrass herself and him by weeping.

"Well, it's not the end, you know. It may seem so at the time, but it never is. In fact, it may very well turn out to be the beginning. It's a great big world out there, my dear, and with your looks and character, I can think of a great many men who will snap you up if they have the chance."

She laughed. "Do you remember that you said that to me once before?"

"I meant it too. Maybe this unhappy experience in Martinique will be a catalyst, ridding you of all those insecurities, the best thing that ever happened. I sound like Pollyanna, I know, and you're probably saying to yourself, 'The old fool doesn't have the least inkling what he's talking about.' But I do know and I'll be very surprised if, not by next week but by next month, you'll agree with me."

Thoughtfully he tapped her manuscript, which lay on his desk. "In the meantime, I'll read this and give you my frank opinion."

The interview over, she hurried back to the apartment and taking Beauregard to a nearby park, sat on a bench while he gleefully chased a squirrel across the greening grass. He barked in frustration when the squirrel, thoroughly enjoying the challenge, eventually grew tired of circling about aimlessly and ended the game by scrambling up a tree, swishing his tail in a triumphant gesture as he balanced precariously on the highest branch.

Well, at least Beauregard has made the adjustment, Carol thought. Warmed by the sunlight, grateful that Charles

Caldwell had been kind enough to give her manuscript a reading, she let the next chapter begin to form in her mind. Realizing that work was her only refuge from the wretched memory of Jules and Martinique, she spent the remainder of the day at her typewriter. When Ann turned the key in the apartment door, announcing that it was after five o'clock, she was astonished that she had become so absorbed in her work that Jules Saint Laurent had been at least temporarily banished.

"Well," Ann declared with a grin, "I was happy to hear the tap of your typewriter. You must have received good news this morning."

"You were right. I can have my old job back if I want it, but best of all Mr. Caldwell has agreed to read my manuscript."

"He's a very nice guy, and he likes you. Also he believes you have talent."

"Did he tell you that?"

"Yes, at the cocktail party I mentioned."

They dined at an Italian restaurant not far down the block from the apartment.

"I won't stay with you for very long, Ann," Carol assured her.

"No hurry. I've even taken a shine to Beauregard. So far, except for a few minor incidents, his deportment has been exemplary."

"So far—" Carol said with a laugh.

She spent the next three days close to the telephone in the apartment, writing steadily, taking Beauregard for brief walks, approaching the state when for long stretches of time, Jules Saint Laurent faded into the background, only to reappear in the lonely, tedious hours of the night.

When the telephone rang and it proved to be Charles Caldwell, she was thankful when he wasted no words on preliminaries. "It's great," he said laconically. "Drop in this afternoon around three and we'll go over the details."

"You remind me very much of your father," Charles Caldwell told her as he motioned her toward a comfortable chair in his office. "He was invariably certain his latest effort was a hideous failure. You're acting remarkably the same, sitting as stiff as a poker, your wide gray eyes filled with anxiety, unable to be convinced that I meant it when I said what you've accomplished so far is great. As I used to tell Carl, have a cigarette or a glass of sherry, but for God's sake relax."

Charles Caldwell had been Carl Spencer's editor from the start to the finish of his career. Carol had always suspected that she had been offered a position in the company largely due to his close relationship with her father. However, sensitive to the fact that it is often difficult to be constantly linked to a famous man, he had in her presence rarely mentioned Carl Spencer's name.

"Have you been working this week?" he asked.

"Constantly. It seems to be falling into place easily, so easily that it worries me."

"You see, that is precisely the answer Carl would have given me. On second thought, it may be a happy portent. You'd be amazed at the number of writers who submit a manuscript to me convinced it will win the Pulitzer prize, and it turns out to be the most awful tripe ever to cross my desk. Modesty becomes you, and as it is close to dinner time, let's go to Lochober's to discuss your work over drinks and a lobster. You look undernourished. I wager you haven't had a proper meal in weeks."

At dinner, she gave him a rough outline of her novel. In return he offered her a healthy advance. "Get away from Boston," he advised. "Go to some quiet spot where you can work undisturbed."

"Nag's Head comes to mind," Carol said, finding it impossible to contain her rising excitement. "My mother and I spent several summers there. In April it will be practically deserted. I could probably rent a cottage for a song."

"Go wherever you wish, but don't forget to give me your address before you leave. You must keep me in touch with your progress. Send along each chapter when it's finished, if you wish."

Later, hurrying back to Ann's apartment, she burst in, unable to withhold her exciting news. Two days later, a cottage at Nag's Head engaged, she packed, rented a car and with Beauregard by her side drove southward.

Her parting words to Ann Sinclair were, "Don't, on pain of death, give my address to anyone. You, Charles Caldwell and my lawyer in New York are the only ones who know where I can be reached. I want to keep it that way."

Not that I expect to hear from Jules, she was thinking as she said good-bye to Ann, but if there is the slightest chance of his trying to contact me, I want to be sure he is thwarted. As a picture of Beau Rivage flashed through her mind, she wondered idly how long it would be before it no longer was hers, and found herself anxious for that day to take place, to sever her remaining link with Jules Saint Laurent and his iniquitous mother.

CHAPTER 22

The cottage was one of a long row of flimsy structures built on slender piers, hidden behind the sand dunes. From her second floor windows, she could see the Atlantic—gray, cold, majestic, so different from the limpid blue waters of the Caribbean, and wherever she was, night and day, she heard the surf as it pounded relentlessly against the shore, its huge whitecapped waves thundering along the beach, leaving swirling eddies of foam in their wake.

She had craved solitude and she found it. At nightfall the surrounding cottages showed no lights and as the icy winds from the ocean penetrated the thin walls, she was thankful for the fireplace in the living room and a plentiful supply of wood.

She wrote swiftly and as her story unfolded to her satisfaction, she found the peace that had eluded her since Martinique. Twice a day, once in the morning and again in the late afternoon, she and Beauregard walked along the beach —Beauregard scampering ahead, circling aimlessly, while she, wrapped in a warm sheepskin coat, trailed behind, savoring the tangy breezes from the sea and the taste of salt on her lips, until a sentence or a paragraph formed in her mind, causing her to scurry back to the cottage before the words she had been seeking escaped.

April, unnoticed, drifted by. May caught her unawares.

Only the opening of a few cottages and the beginning of warmer days warned her that the summer season was fast approaching. Sometimes she opened the door to her memory a crack, wondering when her lawyer in New York would call or write to tell her the sale of Beau Rivage had been consummated, quickly dismissing it as inconsequential, fearful that memories of the terrace above the sea would cause a rush of painful past events best forgotten, the opening of Pandora's box, which once open could not again be closed.

It was the final week in May, the rough draft of her novel finished. Depleted, feeling rather dispirited as she always did when a piece she had been concentrating on was nearing conclusion, one morning she took a blanket from her bedroom, deciding that it was warm enough to stretch out in the sun in blue jeans and a light sweater.

Clambering over a sand dune with Beauregard sporting about some distance ahead, she noticed that the beach was no longer her private preserve, deserted except for the sand pipers and the gulls, who dipped and skimmed over the waves, for today here and there clusters of people were basking in the sunlight.

"Time soon to leave," she murmured, putting on dark glasses and immediately dropping off to sleep.

It was Beauregard who awakened her with an outpouring of excited barks. Opening her eyes, she saw him bounding up and down, his tail in constant motion, impeding the progress of a tall, slender man who, despite the puppy's importunities, was approaching at a rapid pace.

Removing her dark glasses, squinting against the glare of the sun, she recognized Jules Saint Laurent, striding toward her with his easy pace which no one could possibly imitate.

It was far too late to seek refuge in the cottage, to lock the door and refuse to answer.

He stood before her, bending down to pat Beauregard, saying, "Take it easy, old boy." He was smiling, markedly ill at ease as he waited for her to be the first to speak.

"Why did you come?" she demanded. "My lawyer in New York has been instructed to handle the details of the sale of Beau Rivage."

"I don't wish to purchase Beau Rivage."

"Why not, when it has always been your dearest wish?"

"I have no desire to live at Beau Rivage without you."

She laughed, a bitter laugh, unwilling to acknowledge the sincerity of the sorrow in his dark eyes, labeling him a master in the art of seduction, for some unknown reason practicing his charms on her once more. "That's difficult to believe," she retaliated.

"Why did you leave without a word, without waiting for my return? Surely you owe me an explanation for that?" he asked relentlessly.

She shifted uneasily on her blanket. "I should think it must be obvious."

"No, not to me it isn't. To me it remains incomprehensible. My mother told me you stormed into the plantation house one afternoon, declaring it was all over—a mistake, a dreadful mistake. What kind of an admission is that after what had occurred between us? I didn't understand then. I don't understand now. Pride prevented me from coming to you before this for your answer until it reached a point that no matter what your answer, I had to see you. I had to hear the words from you, you alone. Don't you think you owe me that much?"

"Jules," she said wearily, "I don't want to listen to you. I've offered to sell Beau Rivage. What more can you want?"

"I thought you knew."

"I thought I did too—once. But that was when I was in Martinique, naïve, foolish, stupid to give you my love. Whatever you say now, Jules, is inconsequential, yet before you go, there is one misunderstanding I must clarify. I stormed in to see your mother—yes, but not to say I no longer loved you. Instead I asked why I should sign a paper that turned Beau Rivage over to you. I doubt very much if you, with your remarkable ability to smooth out awkward situations, can explain that."

"What paper?"

She stared at him with contempt. "What paper, indeed! The agreement, of course, the agreement Jacques Despard drew up at your instructions. It was clever of you to have him present it after you departed for Guadeloupe. I suppose the two of you were counting on my poor French to fail to grasp your intentions. But my French is not that poor. To me it is incredible that your arrogance led you to believe that I would marry you under such tawdry conditions."

"I took no part in such an agreement," he declared angrily. "What little faith you had in me, Carol, to believe I was capable of such deception. To think you were unwilling to at the very least grant me the chance to deny it."

"At first I did plan to wait for your return," she admitted, shaken somewhat by his denial. "But not after your mother spelled out most clearly what you really thought of me. Some women might be content to become your chattel, not I!"

"I can see," he spoke bitterly, "that my words have not convinced you of my innocence."

"They have not. Never again will I permit you to convince me." Defiantly she scrambled to her feet, ignoring his outstretched hand.

"Why do you suppose I would travel here from Martinique if I were guilty of your charges?" His Latin temperament rising to the surface, his eyes emitted sparks of fury. "If I wanted Beau Rivage, not you, would I have any reason to come here? I have refused your offer. Isn't my refusal proof that your suppositions are entirely false?"

Confused, unsure of her response to his questions, she temporized. "How did you find me?" she asked.

"Through Betsy Johnson. You wrote her a letter from here, and it didn't take long for me to convince her that I loved you, that I had to seek you out. Until today I had no idea that my mother would go to such lengths to drive us apart, to have such a nonsensical paper drawn up by Jacques Despard. I still had faith that you believed in me, that your flight was an impulsive act, because too much had happened too quickly. I thought seeing you face to face would be the answer. Now I realize that you had such little faith in me, you believed my mother's foolish words. Without faith, without trust, there is no future for you and me."

Tight-lipped, he turned from her, ignoring Beauregard's sharp barks of protest. "Be happy in your narrow little world, Carol," he said coldly. "Once I thought you were liberated. Now I see I was wrong."

He strode off down the beach, his hands thrust deep in his pockets.

"Jules," she cried out. "Please don't part in anger. If we can't be lovers, let's not be enemies."

He swung around, smiling in the endearing fashion that had been the prelude to their nights together. "I'm not angry. How can I be angry with someone I find I can't live without?"

They faced each other, tentatively, uncertainly, both wary of making the first move, the first concession. Her defenses fell as, taking the initiative, he reached out his arms to her in supplication. She ran to him. They clung together, their bodies warm, eager, ardent—the charges made, the recriminations, dissolving like an early morning fog on the sea, dissipated by the hot rays of the sun.

"I love you," he said.

"I love you," she replied.

"I love you," a phrase spoken since the beginning of time in countless languages, yet to the man and woman who speak it, it is always fresh, never stale, never tarnished by repetition.

"I have two tickets for Paris in my pocket," he said with a sheepish grin.

"You were that certain of the ending?" she asked, no longer apprehensive of his supreme confidence, accepting it as an integral part of the man she adored.

"No, not this time. I was afraid I had lost you."

Arm in arm they strolled toward the cottage, the bitter words so recently exchanged forgotten. It was as if speaking them had reaffirmed rather than denied their love.

"When does the plane leave?" she asked.

"Two days from now."

"Ah, that gives us time."

"Time for what?"

"Time to draw the shutters and make love."

"Long overdue," he sighed.

"Think of what we have missed because of our silly misunderstandings."

"Never look back, always look ahead," he whispered. "And although I can't promise you the universe, I promise you my love forever. We'll be married in Paris. We will solemnly say 'Oui, Monsieur Le Maire,' as we stand in his presence in his quarters at the Hôtel de Ville. It's a brief ceremony, rather austere, but our ticket to paradise. What more can we ask for?"

Words became irrelevant as they closed the cottage door behind them, leaving Beauregard to flop down on the veranda, thumping his tail disconsolately against the wooden floor.

As Jules had promised, they flew to Paris where their marriage was solemnized at the Hôtel de Ville. They even took Beauregard along on the flight and their honeymoon because they believed, after all, that he had played a major role in their love affair. To their amusement, when they strolled with him through the Tuileries and Luxembourg gardens, he was a sensation, for Parisians are accustomed to chanines with impeccable pedigrees.

They lingered for a time on the Riviera and at last, becoming homesick for Martinique, returned to Beau Rivage, the place where they had met, the place where they had at first been enemies, the place where they had fallen in love.